Rumbullion

Rumbullion

an apostrophe

Molly Tanzer

WORD HORDE
PETALUMA, CA

ISBN 978-1-939905-64-2

A Word Horde Book

Introduction:
The Third Time's The...

After *A Pretty Mouth* appeared in the *Guardian* I was approached by Mark Beech of Egaeus Press, an English publisher of fine limited editions, about putting together a fiction collection. Thus, *Rumbullion, and Other Liminial Libations* (2013), an incredibly sexy hardcover with color endpapers and a print run of just 250. It contained six reprinted short stories and one original novella. My pitch for the novella, *Rumbullion: An Apostrophe*, was "*Rashomon* with fops." It's been seven years, but I still have nothing more to add to that description. After the Egaeus edition sold out, it was reprinted by LFP in 2017, but it soon fell out of print yet again. I'm pleased to once again make it available to the public.

Rumbullion (the *Apostrophe*, not the collection) is still my favorite sort of story to write. There's an anxious frame containing lots of little bits and bobs—a letter, a script, a confession. I especially enjoy the epistolary mode, and its potential to succinctly suggest a bigger world and a larger story.

And speaking of larger stories, fans of one Lou Merriwether, psychopomp, may be surprised when they encounter some familiar faces in *Rumbullion*. I was working on an early draft of *Vermilion* when I wrote *Rumbullion*, and thought it would be funny. It's nice that both books have now found their forever-home here at Word Horde.

—Molly Tanzer, December 2020

I suppose I should have expected an uproar when my mother persuaded the Count of St. Germain to come to Tarrington and play a concert for our friends and family. The man's reputation is as contentious as it is ubiquitous. Who in the civilized world has not heard of St. Germain's alleged miracles, his virtuoso talent on the violin, his strange abilities with gemstones and the dyeing of cloth, his perpetual youth, &c.? The Count has more legends surrounding him than Odysseus, and if half of them be true, St. Germain is better traveled and a good deal more cunning.

That is why I must begin with him—with the Count of St. Germain. But I should note, for the purposes of introducing this account of that strange night, that I no longer hold him accountable for all that occurred. Not wholly. As far as I have been able to ascertain, no one person is entirely to blame.

To keep things organized, I shall begin with the facts. Here is a list of what I can be certain, without doubt, is completely true:

1. The Count of St. Germain agreed, at the invitation of my mother, to come to Tarrington House as our guest and entertain us.

2. St. Germain arrived the morning of 7 June 1743.

3. The weather was extremely clement during his stay—so fine, in fact, that we spent as much time out-of-doors as possible, especially (for me) during the night-time.

4. Our guests included my mother's particular friend Lady Nerissa, my old school friend Cloudsley James, my cousin Vandeleur Welby, lately returned from his Jamaica plantation, and my then-fiancée Phylotha Tydfil Mallory (accompanied by her lady's maid, her sister Jessamine Constantia, and Jessamine's lady's maid

3

Obedience Baker).

5. We were joined by other guests as well, ~~including some who were discovered to have not been invited by anyone~~

No, I cannot claim to be certain of that last bit. This, of course, is my problem! Four points and I have run out of *facts*, even after everything I have done to investigate the myriad strange events of that night. And worst of all, I still have no means to prove beyond a doubt who murdered poor Vandeleur, to name the most fatal enigma.

Thinking back on how this began—*this* meaning my quest to discover the truth—my own naïveté astounds me. I really believed my curiosity could be satisfied by simply asking my guests to recount what they observed that night, each having had, I knew, various experiences; that a representative sample would provide me with perfect insight into the matter. Now, having read, and *re*-read their replies, I find their recollections to be as incomplete and as unsatisfactory as my own.

Perhaps that is what goads me to try to compile and to document all that I know of what happened that night…even if it seems I must indulge in speculation and conjecture to do so, forever dooming my endeavor to inhabit the realm of fiction.

How sad, to admit a defeat before I begin. All I ever desired was to discover what was *true*.

***

I must cease this waffling. I shall never finish if I never begin. Let me try this as an opening, then:

In the early winter of 1742 my father was convalescing close to Flanders, having been struck with pleurisy after taking a bayonet wound to the side. I, too, was ill, suffering from an acute attack of my accursed condition, which prohibited me from attending my mother on her annual and much-anticipated sojourn to London. Hearing this, my mother's good friend, the Lady Nerissa, generously invited my mother to stay with her in town so that neither of them would have the pleasures of the season diminished by staying alone. My mother, who is always in perfect health, was not displeased by this notion. Lady Nerissa always attends the most superior and exclusive of gatherings, and it was at one of these where my mother first encountered the Count of St. Germain. Upon her return she told me the story of that fateful night—how impressed she was by St. Germain's bearing and manners. I listened attentively to all she said, though of course I did not realize how much would come of their chance meeting. At the time I was merely curious about her opinions of someone thought by many to be a magician of the first order, and considered by others to be a notorious charlatan.

Unfortunately, my mother now takes to her bed whenever the Count is mentioned (poor Vandeleur was her sister's only son), so I must here rely on only what I can recall of that conversation. I know she said the Count performed several of his own compositions on the violin for the enjoyment of all, but what else she said about his recital escapes me.

It is what my mother told me of his other entertainment that remains most vividly in my mind. Apparently, the Count was able to remove ten years of age from their hostess' face by means of her swallowing a draught of his own devising, as well as allowing him to rub a second tonic into her temples, around her eyes, and over her teeth. My mother claimed that she saw the woman's wrinkles *drop from her face and into her lap.* (If she mentioned what happened to her hostess' teeth, I cannot recall.) I, of course, expressed some doubt as to the veracity of this, remarking that this feat must have been some sort of clever illusion, but my mother would not agree. Instead, she swore that St. Germain collected the wrinkles with a pair of fine tweezers, stowing all he could find in a jewel-encrusted snuffbox. When I asked why he would want such a memento, she replied the Count had claimed that he always wove women's wrinkles into the bowstrings of his violin, for the blend produced a sweeter tone than horsehair alone.

Fascinated and awed by this, when later that night they sat down to some newly fashionable game called *whist* my mother enquired if the Count would be so kind as to grace us with his presence at Tarrington House for a similar demonstration. But the Count of St. Germain refused her at that time, citing too busy a schedule to promise an appearance anywhere until well after the new year. Mother was understandably disappointed, but chose not to press him.

I believe it was some weeks after that night when my mother met the Count a second time, at a soirée where he was to be merely a guest and not a performer. Even so, my mother witnessed him perform a second, even more astonishing miracle. During dinner, a young man took too large a bite of his cheese-wig and choked on it. His companions were thrown into a state of panic; many attempted to dislodge the offending morsel. When that was not possible, a doctor attempted to revive the lad with smelling salts, but that too failed. The boy died horribly of asphyxiation as his friends watched helplessly on.

Unflustered, the Count shooed all away from the stripling's prostrate form, coolly calling for a bellows and a glass of raspberry cordial. When both arrived, he surrendered his stick-pin, which was set with a large diamond, and dissolved the stone in the fluid. This mixture he administered with a dropper via the nostrils, first tipping back the dead youth's head, and lo! The lad's eyelids began to flutter! Then the Count applied the bellows to his purple, slack mouth and began forcing air into his lungs.

This called the boy fully back to life, to everyone's amazement.

When he had quite recovered the boy reported having dreamed himself walking in a lovely garden that was possessed of every seasonal beauty, when the Count, surrounded by a purple halo, approached him and told him he must come in to dinner. Taking his hand, St. Germain led him to a door, pushed him through— and he awoke much confused to the party all standing over him!

But I digress;[1] what is important is that later that night my mother repeated her request to St. Germain that he attend us at Tarrington. She told him she had no desire other than to enjoy his presence and his talents, and whenever he could come, she would have him. More amenable to her request the second time, the Count agreed to visit in the early summer.

Soon after that St. Germain quit London, and my mother did not hear of him again until he sent word to her, after her return home, asking if the second weekend of June would be acceptable. She was overjoyed at this; I, ambivalent, still skeptical at that time of St. Germain's alleged powers, but eager for some diversion. Though summer in the country affords many pleasures for the solitary man, company is necessary to keep healthy the mind, body, and spirit.

Before I continue, I feel I should reiterate that I do not hold the Count accountable for the general mayhem of that night. Not wholly. And neither do I consider my mother at fault for

1. I would be remiss, however, should I fail here to note that several weeks after the event chronicled above, the boy's mother, when asked about her son's health, was heard to report it better than ever before— though she was much confounded that not two days after her son was called back to life by the Count, the boy shat out St. Germain's diamond, whole again, and seemingly unaffected by its digestive journey. She also said that when she wrote to the Count he declined the bauble's return, and even suggested it might be sold to help the youth's matrimonial prospects. Indeed, the family in question is rich in good name but poor in cash, though how the Count came by that information is anyone's guess. –J.B.

extending the invitation. She could not have known anything like what occurred would occur. Nor do I condemn myself for failing to forbid the man from coming here. I am not prescient, nor am I even particularly perceptive, as I have discovered.

The thing for which I hold myself accountable is having allowed the events of that night to change me, mostly, but perhaps not entirely, for the worse. What a terrible thing to write, I know, but this record of that night is for myself. For my eyes alone. No one need know of my newfound selfishness. Yes—selfishness. I have always prided myself on being a man of sensibility, but the simple act of looking over these letters I sent to my friends mere weeks ago has shown me that is no longer the case. Given the chance, I know in my heart that in spite of what occurred, I would not prevent the occurrences of that night were it in my power to do so.

***

The Lady Nerissa was the first guest to whom I wrote, once I had resolved to uncover all I could about that night. My reasons were these: Lady Nerissa has always been a part of my life; she and my mother were great friends before my mother became Mrs. Bretwynde, mistress of Tarrington, and the lady gained her title through marriage. I have always considered the lady to be possessed of excellent reason as well as temper. Indeed, with my father gone, it was to she whom I applied for advice before proposing marriage to poor Phylotha. (I cannot fault her for her encouragement; she could not have anticipated this recent unpleasantness.) Also, I thought to speak with her first as she was present when my mother made the Count's acquaintance.

Here is the letter I sent to her:

Lady Nerissa
Wuthermoor Hall
Chittlehampton
Devon

My Lady,

I hope this missive finds you in good health. I did myself the pleasure of writing to you in order to thank you for your thoughtful gift of the damson preserves. They have been much enjoyed by everyone in our household; as you know, my father left instructions for all of our own crop to be turned into gin, so without your generosity we should have had to go without. I know my mother plans on repaying your kindness when our bergamot and Spanish oranges are ready to be turned into marmalade, so when the cooler weather comes, expect your basket returned, full once again!

You are too discerning, however, to believe that I would write to you solely in order to compliment your jams and jellies. No, I write to you in regards to the Count of St. Germain. I will be blunt with you, my lady—the night of his concert yet haunts me. I cannot put it out of my head; my mind returns to him whether I am awake or asleep. I confess this to you alone; I have always valued your friendship, and I know you will not judge me, nor will you tell others of what I have written here.

If I could explain my obsession, I would. Perhaps it is the subsequent news, which I am sure you have heard, regarding the dreadful fate of my cousin Vandeleur Welby, which keeps me from forgetting what occurred; perhaps it is the loss of my once-dear Phylotha. Ah, regarding that…I know it is only to be expected that Mr. Mallory will not allow me to see her, but given that she is in no condition to write, nor any of her family to contact me, I have had no news of her at all. Have you heard anything of how she fares, or her future prospects?

Additionally, if you would be so kind, I would appreciate any personal insights you might have regarding the Count of St. Germain and his visit. What did you think of him before your stay at Tarrington? After? What did you see of him, and observe about his effect on others, during that fateful night? My request in this regard is not solely personal; it has been suggested by more than one among my acquaintance that I press charges against the man. I am still formulating my opinion on that matter. While I was in a way wronged by him—or at a minimum, by his choice of entertainments—I feel there are others who have greater cause to complain.

I am once again in need of your discerning judgment. I do hope you will be as generous with your advice as you were with your preserves.

I remain affectionately yours,

Julian Bretwynde

Lady Nerissa replied very quickly indeed:

Julian Bretwynde
Tarrington House
Tavistock
Devon

Oh Julian,

My dear boy, you did yourself a credit in writing to me about this matter. You have always been far too excitable, whereas I cannot remember the last time I shed a sentimental tear or fretted for more than ten minutes about a matter beyond my power to control. I warned your mother about this when you were just a little boy, weeping over the slightest hurt. But she would coddle you, even from the beginning. Why, she threw an absolute fit when it was time for you to be wet-nursed, as if it were not the most natural thing in the world. And now here we are.

While I understand how the unpleasantness which occurred in the wake of the Count's visit might account for your haunted dreams and whatever else, you simply must learn to see things as they are. You have lost a cousin in an unexpected and frankly gruesome way. That is a terrible tragedy—most especially because, from what I hear, you were not mentioned in his will. But as to the other—Miss Mallory, I mean—that is no tragedy. What is bred in the bone will come out in the flesh and all that. You asked for advice, so I advise you to look at things from my perspective; while it may seem unfeeling, trust me: I am thinking of you. Who knows how maudlin thoughts will affect your general health? You are not only delicate in spirit, you know.

Perhaps I am being too hard on you. Certainly you had real feelings for Miss Mallory—which, I would have you recall, was the only objection I had to your proposing to her. It must have been a terrible experience, severing your ties with her and her family, and under such dreadful circumstances. That said, what other choice did you have? At least take some comfort that your decision has been borne out. I have indeed had news of the girl. She has been permanently confined to her rooms for the foreseeable future, and I am not sure if I should tell you more than that. You are so very easily distressed, I believe it may be better for you not to know. Suffice it to say that little Jessamine Constantia has been sent to away to school until Miss Mallory is recovered, or until such a time as a more permanent solution must be entertained.

(Not to digress, but yes, you read that correctly—Jessamine Constantia! At school! Can you imagine? What on earth could she be learning? Well, it is "the mode," for families of that class, I suppose. I would never send a daughter of mine to such a place; then again, I have no daughter.)

Now, as to whether you should press charges against the Count, I cannot see how that would be wise, or even possible. Do you know where he is gone? What would you accuse him of? In what way do you feel you have been wronged by him? Really Julian, if you think rationally about it, he did you a favor. Can you imagine what a misery your life would be had you not been warned of Miss Mallory's "instability?" And what of the children you would have gotten on her? My heart beats a little faster thinking of it. Perhaps you are not so alone in your squeamishness after all.

If you were to send the law after anyone, it should be that repulsive stunted foreigner with the large eyes and impossible-to-pronounce name that your idiotic friend Mr. James invited. Thank goodness you had me, and your mother, and—before everything—Miss Mallory to keep him away from little Jessamine Constantia. She was so enchanted with him it's a wonder he didn't prey upon her innocence when they were alone in the garden together. You never know what a foreign youth will do with a good English girl like Jessamine.

As for my opinions, or insights, or whatever it is you asked about the Count, they have not changed. When I met his lordship in London I found him a charming fellow possessed of no small skill on the violin. Whatever nonsense your mother told you about his magical abilities—Julian, you know I adore Delphia, and always have, but she is *hardly* the woman to be consulted for advice on how to keep one's feet on the ground. As a girl she would always drag me to see fairy circles, get her fortune read at traveling carnivals...you know, that sort of thing. She bought the Count's act as eagerly as a fop buys a new pair of gloves. Surely she told you about their second meeting, the whole affair with the boy and the cheese-wig? When asked, St. Germain claimed he knew the boy had not died completely. I ask you, really now, what does that mean? Is the boy Christ come again? The reason he gave for being sure of this? *The lad's opal ring had not lost its luster.* Apparently there is some peasant superstition that opal rings "die" with their owners! Typically I pay no heed to such nonsense, but some idiot in the party remarked they had heard something about that when reading a history of the Great Mortality. The Count's reply? "Yes, I saw much evidence to support the theory at that time." *At that time!* Indeed! Thus he creates his own legends about his supposed immortality.

I said nothing to discredit the Count on the matter of his having been alive during the reign of Edward III. I could see plainly how my compatriots longed to believe him—most of all your mother, of course, who looked at her own opal ring and cried out.

"What, dear lady, troubles you?" asked the Count.

"My wedding ring," she said, showing him her own opal. "It is still bright—do you think that means he is still alive?" And then she told him all about your dear father's difficulties in Flanders.

The mountebank told her he was certain it was a sign your father was recovering, but at the sight of Delphia's tears of joy I simply had to interject. You may think me cruel, but chicanery of that sort seems even crueler, to my mind.

"My dear Count," said I, "if what you say is true, would not Mrs. Bretwynde's ring indicate her *own* health, rather than that of her husband?"

"My lady," replied St. Germain gravely, "I can offer no opinion on the fairness of God's laws, or man's—or why opals would choose to obey either. But according to both, do not Mrs. Bretwynde *and* her ring belong to her husband?"

That is the sort of man he is! You must understand my irritation is not over being verbally out-fenced—

well, not entirely. It is more that…let me put it like this…when I speak, I *never* claim to be giving more than my own opinion.

And my opinion is: mourn your cousin as you must, find yourself a more suitable bride—preferably one you do not love—and make yourself forget about the whole affair.

With best love, &ct.,

Lady Nerissa

***

I was grateful to the lady for taking the time to write me such a lengthy reply, but her answers did more to arouse my curiosity than satisfy it. Interestingly, my primary objective in contacting her—ascertaining the lady's opinion of St. Germain—was the least engaging part of her response. I was intrigued by the information that Jessamine had been banished to a school…and fascinated by the lady's allegation that a youth had encountered Miss Jessamine before any of the more dreadful events of the night had taken place.

I could intuit the identity of the individual most closely matching Lady Nerissa's description…but, curiously, he—the youth in question, I mean—had told me it was the Lady Nerissa who had bid him come, and not, as the lady had mentioned, Mr. James. Or, I should say, bid his master come. Yet the lady had made no mention of Mr. Absalom Bernard, only his manservant, Dionysios; indeed, she seemed unaware that Dionysios had been there in the service of another. It seemed wisest to conclude that Mr. Bernard, who played such an important role in the events of that night, had *not* been invited by Lady Nerissa—either that, or she had indeed invited him, and by proxy his servant, and was embarrassed to admit it.

These discrepancies nagged at me so dreadfully that for this and other reasons I risked the lady's displeasure by writing to her a second time:

> My Lady,
> Though I hesitate to trouble you again so soon after my last letter, your kindness in writing me so extensively has, regrettably, only whetted my interest. That said, if you would be so generous as to clear up a few uncertainties for me, I am sure I should be able to heed your very good advice of leaving off contemplating the Count's visit. To bolster my claim's credibility, I offer you this: I very much appreciated your insight regarding pursuing legal action against St. Germain, and I have, on the merit of your advice, decided against such a course.
> But it is not in regards to the Count that I write to you; it is Jessamine Constantia. You said that dear little Jessamine has been shipped off to school…I am curious to know where exactly Jessamine has been sent? I have several cousins from lower branches of the family tree who have been exiled to these new-fangled "ladies' schools," and if Jessamine was unaware of a potential connection, and perhaps therefore a friend, I thought it might ease what I am sure must be no small discomfort in being so far from home, and so unexpectedly.
> Additionally as regards Jessamine, as host I feel I must enquire further about this young man who troubled her so. You said the rascal was invited by

Mr. James, an issue I shall certainly take up with Mr. James. And yet…it is so queer, for the only individual who comes close to matching your description (other than Mr. Welby's manservant Chidike) was not a guest, not as such. He was in fact the servant of a gentleman by the name of Absalom Bernard. Surely you remember Mr. Bernard? He was the handsome fellow with the long, salt-and-pepper hair and the impressive if unfashionable moustache, who arrived much later that night than anyone else—and it was he who won the unfortunate card game with my cousin that preceded, and was perhaps the cause of, his untimely death.

Mr. Bernard was attended by a pageboy of manners and youthful beauty, Dionysios Laskaris. Could it have been he to whom you referred when you spoke of Jessamine's near-tragic encounter? Or was it my cousin's man, Chidike? Even more bizarre is that the boy Dionysios told me that *you* had invited Mr. Bernard to our gathering, not Mr. James!

My lady, I do not mention this last to accuse you, of course—merely to make sure we are not speaking at cross-purposes. After all, a villain who would terrorize Jessamine's innocence would surely not balk at attending a party sans invitation!

This has been such a confusing affair. I find myself overwhelmed and in need of more information in order to redress this wrong done to our mutual young friend. I thank you for your patience.

Yours faithfully,

Julian Bretwynde

Lady Nerissa's reply came even more quickly after this second letter:

Julian,

You say you have taken my advice, but it was to forget *every thing* about this affair, not just your desire to pursue legal action against the Count. But as I can hardly fault you for your concern for young Jessamine, I shall tolerate one final discussion of that most regrettable visit.

I absolutely did not invite anyone to your gathering, much less an "Absalom Bernard." I am acquainted with no one of that name, and while you portray him very vividly, I neither met nor saw anyone that night who came anywhere close to resembling such a description. Now, the youth I spoke of must be this person "Dionysios." Vandeleur's man, Chidike, while obviously a villain, is, so far as I am aware, innocent of any crime against Jessamine.

I am truly sorry this incident still bothers you so deeply, but I am glad to see that at the very least you seem to be thinking of matters beyond that night—and beyond yourself. If you know of anyone currently residing at Miss Dulcibella's Academy for Young Ladies, I am sure Jessamine would appreciate the information. From what I hear, her adjustment has been difficult.

You know I consider you a dear friend, Julian, but—speaking of education—please try to remember what Apuleius said about familiarity and contempt. I

ancée; her family has cut me off from any news of her, for the crime of doing my duty to my family. In light of that, please consider delivering the enclosed to Miss Mallory. My future peace of mind depends upon your decision.

Yours in hope,

J.B.

Dear Miss Mallory,

I write to you in the hope that you will do me the honor of assisting me by providing me with some information that might be viewed as sensitive. Due to the recent unpleasantness that has resulted in my total banishment from your family affairs I must beseech you to be the light that shines in the darkness of my knowledge of any subsequent changes to your sister's unfortunate condition.

Oh, Jess. I can't carry on like that, not with you. You and I have always been such good friends, have we not? My estrangement from the Mallorys has been terrible for a number of reasons, but I speak the truth when I tell you that I count the loss of your company foremost among my complaints. To whom, now, can I speak about novels of the day? Who will argue with me regarding the nuances of the rules for Ombre? And as for the gardens, they are wanting for a brave explorer to seek out dragons' dens and pixie-haunts. You are sorely missed, "St. Georgiana."

I had no knowledge you had been sent away to school until a mutual acquaintance informed me—that is how little I have heard of you and your family since that night. I hope you will understand that is why I must attempt such a desperate gambit in order to ascertain some knowledge of your situation, and of course, that of your sweet sister. Please, Jessamine Constantia Mallory, tell me of Phylotha. How does she fare? Has there been any improvement? Do you hold out hope that she will ever fully recover? Do you know if any charges have been pressed against her? Has she has mentioned me, or given a sign she recognizes my name?

I am sure when you received this letter you expected the above questions. But I must ask you for one other favor. You are not the first to whom I have written in my concern for Phylotha. No, my first correspondent—she who let me know where you were—also mentioned *you*, dear Jess. It was brought to my attention that you had been in some way disturbed by a guest at my home that same night. When my mother, your sister, and the Lady Nerissa saw fit to remove you from the evening's entertainments, I did not at the time realize you had had prior dealings with the youth Dionysios. Apparently he approached you earlier in the day and interfered with your enjoyment of the pleasures afforded by our summertime gardens at Tarrington.

As this report amounts to mere canard without your corroboration, I would like to hear your own account of what happened. Please be honest with me. If you have been wronged in some way, as your host I feel it is my duty to redress the situation, however belatedly.

I fear my name and person may be loathsome to

you, but I sincerely hope your knowledge of my character, as well as the memory of our once-close acquaintance, will convince you that I am, despite everything, worthy of a few moments of your time. I anxiously await your decision. Pray do not make me wait too long.

Your servant,

Julian Bretwynde

***

As I looked for Jessamine's reply, I was temporarily distracted by a missive from Mrs. Welby. While at the time the information it contained seemed to shed little additional light on the events of the night which I have been diligently chronicling, I am including our exchange as it proved, in the end, to be relevant.

> Mr. Bretwynde,
> Thank you for your condolences with respect to the passing of my husband. These last few weeks have been a trying time, as you might well imagine. Losing Vandeleur so suddenly has left me inconsolable; losing our Jamaica incomes have left us very nearly penniless. Without that plantation, while I believe we will be able to retain our London dwelling and the house in Liverpool from which I now write, as well as both carriages and the better part of our stable, I have been informed by my lawyer there is no hope for our apartments in Port Royal, nor the house in Calais, nor our Sav-la-Mar rum distillery, nor our stake in the Antilles Royal Sugar Company, nor several other concerns.

But I know you did not write to hear me pour out my heart regarding my compromised finances. No, you wrote me for a different reason, and while I was not surprised to receive your letter, I was taken aback by its contents.

First and foremost, I have no knowledge of any man called Absalom Bernard. Our plantation, Nineveh, was lost in a card game, yes, but to a Mr. Silvanus Blofeld of Bristol; he sent all the necessary documents with his young servant Teyssandier Vicars to collect the deed of ownership before Vandeleur's corpse had even been returned to me. That servant! Before I met him, I would have thought it unthinkable that beauty such as his could disguise such cruelty! How I begged and pleaded with the youth, Mr. Bretwynde, citing my husband's hot temper, his having been extremely persuadable whilst drinking, his excessive love of betting, as all being reasons why this "Silvanus Blofeld" should leave off with his claim and spare a widow from poverty.

Mr. Vicars, however, would not be persuaded to show any mercy—nor did he express a modicum of sorrow over beggaring me. No, he looked at me with the calmest, most unfeeling eyes I ever beheld and went away with all he came for. That we live in times when such villains walk among us!

After being so coldly taken advantage of, how could I ever dream of accusing a man with whom I have had no dealings, this Absalom Bernard, of murdering my husband? You ought to be more careful about making such claims as you did in your letter. It is obvious that awful creature Chidike was the perpetrator. Are you at all aware of the savage nature of the crime? Surely you are not, if you think a gentleman could do such terrible things. Well, as *I* have not been spared the details of this terror, neither shall I spare *you*.

As you know, Vandeleur departed early from Tarrington House, no doubt to return to me, knowing as he did that I was yet suffering from a difficult parturition. Whilst they rested by the side of the road in a meager hut meant for weary travelers, Chidike attacked and overcame my Vandeleur. My hand trembles as I write, but that savage cut out Vandeleur's throat, bled him dry, removed both his arms and, even ghastlier, *made a meal of them*. They found the *bones*, Mr. Bretwynde, the bones of his arms, and the remains of a spit over a fire.

That is why I cannot believe a gentleman committed this crime. Slaughter, dismemberment, cannibalism—he even mistreated Vandeleur's favorite horse, though not as severely as Vandeleur himself. I mention this only because the noble beast had been left to its own defenses, and when it was found two days later, the creature was nearly dead with fatigue, exposure, and exhaustion.

No, while I am certain your desire to advocate for Chidike does you some sort of credit, your claim that he had no reason to desire Vandeleur's death, is, I'm sorry to say, entirely wrong. Chidike, you see, was part of Mr. Blofeld's winnings. Given that Vandeleur had often told Chidike he would never sell him, the villain clearly desired to revenge himself upon my husband, and attempted an escape, all to avoid being given over to a new master.

That is all I have to say on the matter of Chidike, but not all I have to say to *you*. Mr. Bretwynde. Though you may think me impertinent, please forgive a widow these words: I hope you will learn from Vandeleur's foolishness and never again play cards for high stakes, especially whilst drinking. Let my suddenly reduced circumstances be a lesson to you. Put your family before pride, and your livelihood before pleasure. Some men, among whose numbers I must count my deceased husband, never think beyond the moment when they're drinking wine and carousing with friends—and yet, had he shown more wisdom, more thoughtfulness, he might have considered just how many he placed at risk when he so frivolously wagered away his plantation.

With sincerity and respect,

Petronella Welby

What can be said regarding my sentiments in the wake of reading this letter? At first I felt only confusion, for of course "Teyssandier Vicars," the cold-eyed young servant, must be Dionysios if he had been in possession of documents that would yield Nineveh to this "Silvanus Blofeld." But *why*, I wondered should either of them have adopted another name in the short time between leaving Tarrington, and whenever this exchange with Mrs. Welby occurred? Mr. Bernard had fairly won the bet that gained him Vandeleur's Jamaica holdings. Unless he had been using a false name whilst a guest in my house, for some inscrutable reason of his own, there seemed no profit in falsifying his identity—not at either point, that I could see. It was very strange indeed.

As I read further into Mrs. Welby's letter, however, I was overcome by another emotion, one that pushed to the side all thoughts of Dionysios and his master. I was appalled by her description of Vandeleur's death; I had heard nothing more specific than that the murder had occurred. It was shocking to imagine such an outrage being committed by anyone against his fellow man—but the idea that it could have been *Chidike* shocked me all the more. Why, so often had Vandeleur mentioned how he trusted his manservant's judgment better than his own that I had once remarked he might do worse than send the man to Oxford to learn the law; surely the expense would be paid for in no time by the amount he would save on his solicitor's fees.

And yet, like everything else that had come of my mother's invitation to the Count of St. Germain, nothing seemed quite right about Mrs. Welby's description after the fact. I had been present when the fateful wager was made, and Chidike had not been at stake—quite the opposite, actually. Here is how I remembered the scene, which began after yet another hand had been concluded in Mr. Bernard's favor:

VANDELEUR: (With mild, but amiable irritation) My God, but you're a lucky whorseson. Too lucky. I must withdraw myself from any further betting this evening, I think, lest I lose more hours of my time being lectured when I return home to my wife.

MR. BERNARD: (Amused) Ah, there you have it, my friends—why I shall never marry. I enjoy my life and liberty too much to yield possession of either to another.

VANDELEUR: (More hotly) What can you mean by that, I wonder?

MR. BERNARD: Only what I said. No offense was intended, Mr. Welby. For reasons of your own, you chose to marry; I choose not to, for the same.

VANDELEUR: I meant your intimation that I have given someone else authority over my life.

MR. BERNARD: Was it an intimation? Surely I was simply repeating your own words. You yourself said when you return home to your wife, you—

VANDELEUR: (Very angry now) I thank you to leave my wife out of this!

MR. BERNARD: As you like.

VANDELEUR: I am my own master, sir!

MR. BERNARD: I should never have doubted it, except by your own admission.

VANDELEUR: Then let me show with a deed how you misconstrued my words. I shall play one more hand with you, Mr. Bernard, and for high stakes, too!

MR. BERNARD: How high?

VANDELEUR: As high as you like! I cannot imagine you could name an amount I could not match.

(Here I attempted to intercede, feeling Vandeleur was backing himself into a corner with all his large talk. Drink, I was certain, was contributing to his bravado, and Mr. Bernard was being deliberately provoking. Ah, before I proceed, in order to give the most precise picture of this moment I should note that the Count of St. Germain backed my position, as did Cloudsley James, attempting to dissuade the gentlemen from continuing to speak hasty words, but they would not listen.)

VANDELEUR: Name your wager, Mr. Bernard, and I shall match it. Take care it is valuable. I would not want you to find cause, later, to further impugn my courage.

MR. BERNARD: Well, Mr. Welby, if you are determined to bet as magnificently as possible, then I must wager the dearest thing in my possession: *Dionysios*.

VANDELEUR: I cannot imagine your catamite is particularly

valuable. I have traveled, and am as much a man of the world as you are. His type are common enough.

MR. BERNARD: (Without seeming to have taken the slightest offense) Dionysios, do oblige me and recount the hands we have been dealt this evening? In order, and for each player. There's a good boy.

(To the amazement of all, the youth was able to recite the contents of every hand shown since he had joined us. It was an astounding demonstration of memory. Vandeleur was clearly as impressed as the rest of us, though less willing to admit it.)

VANDELEUR: A very engaging parlor trick, but how shall I estimate its value?

MR. BERNARD: It is more than a parlor trick. Dionysios has the ability to remember anything perfectly, but most especially numbers. I never bother to retain anything anymore; why should I, with such a servant in my employ? He keeps my engagements straight for me, remembers the combinations to all my various safes—I say, should I mention that? Well, as we are both gentlemen I surely don't have to worry about you using the knowledge he carries against me...if you should win.

VANDELEUR: I, too, value my manservant. I shall bet Chidike against your Dionysios. You'd be getting a deal, should I lose; he's well-educated and insightful.

MR. BERNARD: Oh, no *no*. While I'm sure your Chidike is quite excellent, Dionysios is the most valuable thing in my possession. He has been employed by many; most of his employers have been nobility, oh! The secrets he carries in his little pretty head...it is quite dizzying to consider. And while he may never reveal them, for that would be unethical, he has used his knowledge to, let us say, *advise me* when it comes to making certain decisions, business or otherwise.

VANDELEUR: (Clearly very interested) You don't say. Well,

then, I'll wager my rum distillery on Sav-la-Mar. I bought it several years ago, so it is producing finely aged spirits as well as raw at this point.

MR. BERNARD: But is it the most valuable thing in your possession?

VANDELEUR: No, that would be Nineveh.

MR. BERNARD: Indeed? What is—

VANDELEUR: My plantation.

MR. BERNARD: Well, that seems reasonable. I shall take your bet—your plantation for my Dionysios. If you win, you'll have no cause to complain, I assure you...

And yet Vandeleur *did* complain, loudly, when he yet again lost to Mr. Bernard. He complained of the unfairness of the cards, his misfortunes, his wife, his lot in life, his newfound poverty, his willingness to risk all to obtain "a gossipy madge." Why, he even complained of his companions, as if we had all not actively attempted to dissuade him from his foolishness! Nothing anyone said could convince him to calm himself, until the Count of St. Germain intervened by suggesting an entertainment in the garden—one that required Mr. Welby's help specifically.

Thus began *my* misfortunes—but I must not get ahead of myself.

I was writing of my confusion upon reading Mrs. Welby's accusation of Chidike. Despite her insistence that only a savage could commit such an act, it nagged at me that she had had the details of the wager wrong. Surely Chidike, who had said so often that never returning to Nineveh would be too soon, would not slaughter and consume his master for frittering away the one thing that would call him thence! No, I could not believe he had motivation to commit the murder.

As I doubted my opinion would do much to persuade Mrs.

Welby to reconsider her theory of the crime, I resolved to visit Chidike and learn from him what I could. But as I began to plan a journey to Chittlehampton, I experienced such a severe attack of rheumatics (which often plague me, a symptom of my overall condition). All I could do was beg Sukey to once again allow me to dictate a letter, this time to Chidike's jailers, begging them to postpone his trial until I had time to speak with them, for I was ill, but (I confess I exaggerated) possessed of evidence that could clear Chidike's name.

As I languished, wasting away in a laudanum haze and bored out of my skull, a ray of light penetrated my grey dolor: a letter from Jessamine. Her response diverted me; the girl had much to say, all of which interested me greatly:

> Julian! You were the last person in the world I ever expected to hear from during my exile, but I am so grateful you wrote to me in my misery. How clever you were to ensure your letter ended up in my hands, and not burned in the headmistress' fireplace! I am certain, had you simply addressed it to me, that Miss Dulcibella would have read it all, and—well, probably she would not have burned it, she would have sent it to my mother, and God knows what would have happened then. Given her record, she probably would have had me flogged and you drawn and quartered. Hateful creature.
>
> You may wonder why I am being so free in what I write to you, but it is simple enough for me to escape detection—far simpler than what you had to contrive! Every third Wednesday we "young ladies" (fie!) are allowed a half-day to ourselves; most of us stroll down to the village for exercise and to see if

there is anything new in the shops that we would like to waste our pocket-money on, ribbons and things, you see. I simply fell away from the group, posted the letter, claiming it was from Obedience to Sukey (hence the address) and *la!* There you have it.

I know first you will be wanting news of my sister; sadly, I have little that is good to report. Despite being leeched so often I'm amazed she has any blood left in her, treated with violent purges that have more than once left her too weak to sit up for days at a time, starved, beaten, and finally locked away, whatever has "gotten into her" as Mother puts it, is still refusing to get out. It really is beyond anything imaginable. You enquired if she had asked for you—Julian, she barely speaks in sentences on the rare occasions I am able to talk to her, for she sleeps during the day and comes awake at night. Unless compelled by awful violence she will not groom herself beyond basic bathing, nor will she put on anything other than the dress she was wearing the night of your ball, even though it is tattered, stained, and has been torn so dreadfully that you can see her knees below the hem! It's positively indecent; even I think so.

And all that is not the worst of it, I am sorry to say. Oh Julian, you will not like to hear this, but Phylotha's madness goes far beyond dishevelment and bad manners. Something is deeply wrong with her, more than the normal sorts of madness one hears of. You know what I mean, the tales one hears from those who have taken tours of Bethlehem, or rumors about someone's eccentric cousin that had to be disinherited. Well, Phylotha's illness is far

ghastlier. Ever since that night she has become ter-
rifically strong and fast—well, when not weakened
by medical treatments. She will eat only meat and
drinks only water, wine, or milk, which she likes best
of all. The worst of her symptoms, however, is that
she will not suffer any man to come near her, from
a doctor to little Dog Friday, whom you know she
raised from a pup. When anything male comes near
her she begins to wail and cry the most outrageous
of sounds, you-*hoo* you-*hoo*, over and over again, and
tries to attack them with her bare hands. The first
time Dr. Farsdale came to visit she bit him on the
calf of the leg before we knew to bind her arms to
her sides.

Wild female creatures are Phylotha's only welcome
companions now; she has been allowed to sit alone
in the gardens several times, restrained and in her
wheeled chair of course, and each time her attendant
has returned, they've caught sight of her with some
new-tamed thing about her. The first time it was two
fox kits playing about her feet; the second, a still-
dappled fawn had its head in her lap, like the strangest lady and the unicorn tapestry you could imagine.

No one, at least in my hearing, has given a name to
whatever is wrong with Phylotha. Given how poorly
traditional cures have worked, however, I would not
be surprised if they called for an agent of the Lord
to try his hand with my sister, though who knows
how *that* will work out. Badly, I suspect. She will
have to sweat or bleed or void herself of whatever
ails her. If not, I fear for her future liberty. And even
if she does recover, well, we have had a letter from

Mr. James' solicitor, saying that Mr. James has been "kind enough" to agree to seek *only* financial restitution for his "physical and mental anguish" until Phylotha recovers. Kind! Well, I'm sure I don't need to spell out what I think of *that*. If demanding a grieving family pay five hundred pounds is kindness, goodness knows what cruelty is. I won't say it would be better if my sister never recovers, but I shudder to think what future "kind" requests await if such happens.

So that is all the news I have regarding my sister's misfortunes. It is very terrible, and while my parents are stubbornly refusing to see your side of the matter, I understand why you broke things off with Phylotha. As her sister, I worry the same taint lies within me; how could you willingly, knowingly marry and have children with her? After all, even if you truly wanted to go ahead with the marriage, she would very likely attack you the moment she saw you standing at the altar!

I have said enough on the matter to last a lifetime, but cannot yet conclude this missive. I am eager to disabuse you of your notions, no doubt planted by that insufferable busybody Lady Nerissa, regarding what happened between myself and Denys, or as you called him, Dionysios. How bizarre to see his full name written out, and hear him called by it! Why, of course I know that was his name, but he prefers his friends to call him Denys.

If I am correct, and you did hear about Denys "interfering with my enjoyments" (or however you put it) from Lady Nerissa, you heard some sort of dreadfully dire account, likely with my very nearly ending up ruined—and yes, I know what that means—by a wicked youth with an alluded-to taste for stealing virtuous maidenheads from those possessed of them. Well, that is not any sort of accurate portrayal of Denys. No; like me, Denys was simply invited to a party less interesting than an average afternoon spent at home, and therefore forced to make his own fun.

Yes, most surely think fourteen is an age when a boy should be nearly a man, interested in smoking and drinking port wine and discussing whatever it is men discuss—and surely there are boys of that age who yearn to be included in such rituals. But Denys was not one of their number. I am in no great rush to be invited—meaning required—to do everything with grown women, and in that regard Denys was as kindred a spirit as I have met in my life.

That is how we met, come to think of it. The morning of your party, which was gloriously warm and sunny, practically begging to be enjoyed, I had fled my bedroom by—well, I suppose I should apologize to you for ruining your lovely sheets by knotting them together so tightly, but really, it is the only way to ensure you won't plummet to your death when climbing out a window. I'm sure you will understand, dearest Julian. But that is beside the point—after Phylotha bustled in to tell me that I had best bathe and make myself ready for breakfast, I made as quick an exit as I could in order that I should be able to enjoy some part of my day.

Your grounds are so extensive I knew it would be difficult to find me if anyone even bothered to go looking once they saw the evidence of my escape. Even so, I did not linger in any one place, in order to be even more difficult to track (unless they set the hounds after me), wandering through the cottage garden and along the banks of your ponds. Eventually I came upon the shed where the games equipment is stored; it not locked, so I got out some quoits. After pounding in the hob—thankfully the earth was still quite moist from where the game had been set up the night before—I was doing rather well when I heard someone stage-cough behind me.

I whirled 'round, and there was Denys—I didn't know he was called Denys then, I suppose, so I should say *there was a pageboy*—leaning against a tree. He grinned at me when he saw how startled I was by his presence! I blushed as red as an apple, for I had not dressed. I was in less than *dishabille*, and very sweaty. But I have found it is always better to bluster through a strange situation than run from it.

"Who are you," I said, "and what are you doing there?"

"You're good at that," he said, instead of answering my questions. "Can I play with you?"

"If you like," I answered, feigning more boldness than I felt. "Are you any good?"

"I don't know," he said. "I've never played before."

"Never played at quoits!"

"No."

I was more than a little surprised; I thought *every-one* played quoits. After all, even the lowliest among us can hammer a stick into the ground and try to throw a hoop around it.

"You'd better come over here if you want to learn," I said. "You won't get the hang of it lurking beneath that tree."

The boy laughed, and all of a sudden he was beside me. I never saw anyone or anything so swift, not even a spooked colt. He leaned down, grabbed a quoit, and promptly dropped it.

"They're heavy!" he exclaimed.

"They're made of iron," I said. "What did you expect?"

"How could I know what to expect if I've never played?"

He had a point. "I can get you the children's set if you like," I teased. "They're made of rope."

"I'll try to manage." He picked up the ring again, squinted, stuck out his tongue, and tossed. It fell into the soft earth half a foot from the hob.

"Not bad," I said.

"Let me try again." This time his quoit caught the edge of the hob, spun around a few times, and then rattled to the ground. He looked pleased with this triumph.

"Nicely managed," I said, more than a little impressed. "Not everyone gets the hang of it so quickly."

"It's fun," he said.

We took turns after that, not really keeping score, though I know by the end of the morning I was ahead by three. We had a lovely time together. He was so very amiable, never afraid to laugh when he failed to score and always ready with applause when I triumphed; he was more gentlemanlike in his manners than many a youth in a brocade coat. He never once commented on my state of undress or said anything untoward. And lest my praise lead you to draw the same conclusions as Lady Nerissa, let me assure you that my feelings toward Denys were in no way romantic. How could they be? We were of a height, of an age, shared similar opinions on issues of the day, novels, sport (as I discovered through our conversation); also, he, like me, professed a love of being out of doors more than anything else. We were too similar, save for his lesser skill at quoits, and who but a fool feels adoration for his reflection in the mirror? When I fall in love, it will be with someone very different, so that we will always have something to say to one another beyond, "yes, I feel the same!"

When we had had enough exercise and sunshine we retreated to sit in the shade underneath a tree. Only then did the boy ask my name. When I told him who I was, and that I was staying at Tarrington House in order to enjoy the Count of St. Germain's performances, he fell silent for a moment. Withdrawing a flask from his coat pocket, he took a swig, and offered it to me. I sniffed—it was a spirit of some sort. I took an experimental sip. It tasted of pears.

"Have you seen him perform yet? The Count?" he asked, after I returned his liquor, and he took another draught.

"Yes, last night."

"What did he do?"

I had escaped listening to his violin recital by running away when no one was looking, but at dinner the Count had given us a demonstration of his more interesting abilities. I told the boy—whose name I still did not know—how the Count had professed to be able to know things about a person's past and future by what dishes he selected at the table.

"Was he successful? Did he do well after making such a claim?"

"Yes," said I, taking a longer drink when he proffered his flask to me a second time. It was good and I was thirsty. "He knew all sorts of things. He knew that earlier this week I had lied to my mother."

"Very good. What did you lie about?"

"After promising her I'd work hard if I was allowed to take my embroidery outside by the lake, I went bathing all morning."

"Remarkable." Returning his flask to his coat pocket, the boy wrapped his arms around his knees and sighed as if his heart would break.

"What is it?" I asked.

"Do you think it is true—all they say about the Count of St. Germain?"

"I don't know *all* they say about the Count," I replied.

"They say he is two thousand years old, or older, and that he is an alchemist who possesses the formula for the elixir of life."

The boy's tone, which I can only describe as world-weary, made me wonder if he had a reason for asking if he thought such outlandish and in my opinion ridiculous legends could be true.

"Those are astonishing claims," said I. "Why are you so interested? Are you seeking the secret of immortality?"

He looked at me keenly. "I seek nothing except to

serve my master, Absalom Bernard," he said. "That is my sole occupation."

"You're not serving him now; you're sitting under a tree with a girl."

"With a friend, I hope." He smiled. "I had not expected to make one this night. But worry not—my master has yet to arrive. I was sent ahead with his luggage, and after setting his room to rights, chose to occupy my time before dinner wandering the gardens."

"Will you be at dinner if your master is not yet arrived?"

"Yes—one way or another."

Before I could ask what he meant, I heard a screech and then my mother swooped down upon me like a hawk.

"Jessamine Constantia Mallory! How *dare* you!" She yanked me to my feet by my ear. "I've been looking *everywhere* for you! Just look at you—you haven't bathed, you haven't dressed, your hair is in a state!" Only then did she notice my companion. "And who are you with!" she cried.

Already on his feet, the boy bowed. "My name is Dionysios Laskaris, if it please you, madam. I serve Mr. Absalom Bernard, a guest of the Bretwyndes not yet arrived. I meant no offense, I came upon Miss Mallory in the garden and, thinking it ungallant to allow her to remain unchaperoned, I offered her my protection."

"Your protection!" exclaimed my mother. "Indeed! And I wonder what you mean by that? Well, I never—I shall speak to your master of your impertinence and see that you are whipped soundly for preying upon my daughter!"

"Mama," I said, "he didn't prey upon me. We played a game—"

"A game!"

My mother slapped me across the face and dragged me away, still protesting the innocence of the youth whose name I had just learned.

You might imagine that my mother and her flock of hens kept a close watch on me for the rest of the day; Phylotha was also assigned as a guard, not only of my physical body, but of my voice. Any time I attempted to leave a place where I was commanded to be, or opened my mouth to speak, I was prevented from doing so—even when I tried to protest the disreputable behavior of that aforementioned, *awful* Mr. James toward Denys at dinner. I cannot believe you voluntarily associate with a rake of such unapologetic boldness; I hope you spoke to him. Surely you saw Mr. James attempt to pull Denys onto his lap and kiss him? If not, I saw his pass with my own eyes, and if you are truly concerned with guest-host relations, you will forbid Mr. James from attending more gatherings at Tarrington.

But that is neither here nor there; what I mean to say is that when everyone met to play cards and drink, was I able to catch Dionysios' eye and draw him away from his master. We retreated to a secluded corner of the drawing room to speak.

"I am sorry we were so rudely interrupted," I said. "Though I am not sorry to have finally learned your name."

"Did I not introduce myself?" he asked. "My apologies. But Miss Jessamine, won't you call me Denys? It is much less formal, as is right between friends."

"I will call you whatever you like," I replied, "but you remind me of your namesake more than a little."

"I hope not," he said soberly. "St. Dionysios of Zakynthos is always portrayed as an old, bearded man—even worse, he was pious, gave all his worldly goods away, and favored seclusion and contemplation of God to anything else. I, as I hope you can see, am youthful and handsome, I love wearing fine clothes and sleeping in a soft bed, and enjoy company to isolation. Well, *some* company…"

I giggled. "I did not realize," I said. "I thought you had been named for the god—who is, if I recall, known for being beautiful, youthful, and social."

"A common enough mistake." He looked pointedly at where my mother sat, chatting with several friends. "Will you get into further trouble if we are seen engaged in conversation? I should hate to cause you or your family further distress."

"Well, you and I aren't alone—a terrible sin, apparently. Surely not even my mother could see something untoward in our becoming further acquainted. We are on our feet, after all, giving the illusion of propriety."

"Is it only the illusion?"

Before I could come up with a sufficiently witty reply, we were interrupted by a burst of hearty laughter from the table where Denys' lately-arrived master Mr. Bernard played cards with the Count of St. Germain, you, Mr. James, and another whose name

I cannot recall, but who was attended by an African servant. Mr. Bernard drained his glass and cast about for a moment, searching for someone to refill it, until the next hand was dealt and he had to return his attention to the game.

Denys sighed. "It is frustrating, is it not, to be under the rule of someone else? To have your decisions made for you?"

"Frustrating, but unavoidable," said I. "At least, for me."

"What's that?"

"As a man—young or not—you have more freedom than I could ever imagine."

"You think so, do you?" he asked, a trifle warmly. The contrast of brightness and shadow cast by all the candles had made him look mysterious and beautiful; now he looked like a devil. I took a step back, surprised by his appearance and aggressive tone. "Even if my sex is allowed greater liberty, what of my station? A young woman of means such as yourself has, to my mind, far less to complain about than those destined to serve due to low birth."

I didn't wish to quarrel with him, but I could not help it. I never can.

"Indeed!" I said. "Well, I shall keep that in mind if my father decides I shall be wed to some terrible ancient monster with deep pockets but no passion. I imagine it will comfort me greatly. Just promise me that when you fall in love and are able to marry whomever you choose, you'll spare me a thought as you say your vows?"

Denys opened his mouth, then shut it, bowed, and

straightened. "Madame," he said, "I have been too long away from my duties. Please excuse me—I must attend my master."

All my pique vanished. "I've offended you—I'm sorry," I said quickly. "I have an argumentative nature, everybody says so, I don't mean to be rude. Please, let me—"

"Madame," he interrupted, and left me.

"Denys!" I cried.

And that, Julian, was my downfall. A hush fell after my yelp; in my heedless distress, I was overheard. Almost quicker than the lad left me, Phylotha was by my side.

"You must learn to control yourself, *Jessamine*," she hissed, half-pulling, half-dragging me toward the door."

"But—" Denys had joined his master, and even with Phylotha's rapid ushering me from the room I could observe the card-playing had entered a more serious phase; no further bursts of levity came from that corner of the room.

"You stupid girl," she said, after we were in the hall. "You need to think of your reputation. What will you do if you cannot marry?"

"I'm thirteen!"

"You think you have all the time in the world. Well, dear sister, maybe you will think back on this conversation twenty years from now, when you are alone, and the life before you consists of watching Mama and Papa age, serving them tea, entertaining their increasingly elderly company, and then, when they pass on, you'll go...where exactly? Are you certain our second cousin will let you stay, when he inherits? Can you promise I shall not die in childbed, and there will be a place for you here?"

Her argument hearkened back to what had caused the row between Denys and myself. I allowed myself to be led away, and put early to bed.

This letter has become very long, and I have taken too long to write it. I assume you will want less news faster, given your concern for Phylotha, so I will conclude now. I assure you that knowing as I do your sentiments toward my sister, and the refusal of my parents to enlighten you as to her situation, I will endeavor to get further reports to you when I receive any.

Be well, dear Julian—

Jessamine Constantia

***

When I began this endeavor, I desired this book to contain, in the end, as truthful an account of the night of St. Germain's concert as could possibly be produced. And yet, even having dedicated so much time to this project—dedicated *myself*, if I may; a hierophant to veracity—I hesitate to confess what comes next, even if only to myself. What individual delights in describing his own weakness, his poor behavior? His anger—especially that of an irrational, impotent nature? But I must do it, for to leave out my feelings and actions would necessitate leaving out how I discovered the last part of Jessamine's letter. If this chronicle is for me, why should I lie to myself? I may not be the wisest of men, but surely I am capable of discerning my own falsehoods. No, I must plunge ahead, no matter how uncomfortable it makes me.

Reading Jessamine's letter made me as furious as I can ever remember being in the whole of my life. I was tormented by what it contained. When I requested the girl write to me, never did I expect to read such terrible things as her missive contained. It was outrageous. Unthinkable!

Denys! Dionysios told the chit to call him Denys? That he preferred to be called that by his *friends!* What, then, was I? Did we not spend much of that fateful night together, and in a most companionable fashion? Did I not hear, from his own lips, that leaving Tarrington hurt his heart most abominably, for he had found "a true compeer" at long last? Was he talking of *Jessamine* when he said that? But no—the sweetness of his voice—the way he looked into my eyes—the gentleness of his touch on my thigh! Even with what came after, I still believed in his love—that is, until I read Jessamine's letter.

I was not to be consoled. Still in a haze from the tincture of opium I was taking for my condition I stormed about my father's study, cursing, vowing revenge, being, I can admit now, rather ridiculous. I resolved to burn Jessamine's letter, to revenge myself on her—a mere girl! I dreamed of finding Dionysios, wherever he had gone to, and demanding at swordspoint or gunpoint some justification for his inconstancy!

The shame of it all; I blush, writing this.

When the anger had mostly passed, then did the tears come. Oh, Dionysios! You bewitched me, with your youthful beauty, with your warmth, honesty, candor, and humor! You forced me, though gently, to acknowledge a part of me that I had never before known existed…but I must move on, for so I did.

Of course I had observed what Jessamine pointed out in her letter, as regards Cloudsley's rude treatment of Dionysios during dinner. I found his behavior beyond ungentlemanlike, just as she said, and though Jessamine did not see it, I told Cloudsley so—though to little effect, as shall be revealed presently.

Truth be told, I had noticed Dionysios even before my old school friend began to pay him such unwonted attentions, for he was a youth of surpassing attractiveness and noble bearing. That, and even in a large house such as Tarrington, a servant without a master has a difficult time going unnoticed, being the most unnatural creature in society.

But given the severity of Cloudsley's assault, I felt I owed Dionysios more than an apology, hence my introducing myself to him. My friend had clearly much embarrassed the boy when he pulled him so roughly into his lap and attempted to kiss him, especially as my friend's heedless sport caused Dionysios to spill wine everywhere, spattering many, including the Count of St. Germain. The eloquence of the youth's speech and comportment fascinated me when, after writhing away, he excused himself in order to procure some vinegar. (The Count kindly assured him that, being much interested in textiles, he would get his own stains out, and not to worry.) Thus, when the ladies had gone off to gossip away their evening, I took the boy aside and offered for him to sit at table with the gentlemen, and take a glass of port and, if he wished, a cigar.

"Thank you, sir, but I would feel more than a little presumptuous," said Dionysios, softly, sweetly. "It is not my place."

"Damn *place*," I replied, surprising myself. "If you will not sit with us, I shall insist you take a turn with me in the gardens."

Dionysios hesitated, then, glancing over at the company, assented. "I would feel worse taking you from your guests," he said. "If you insist, I will sit with you. But no cigar, please."

"Suit yourself," I replied. "Port?"

The boy joined us, where he was welcomed by all (though Cloudsley, miffed at the lad's rebuff of his advances, was not particularly warm). Sipping at his glass of port, he said but little—until, that is, the subject turned to immortality. As Jessamine noted, that topic fascinated him.

Ironically enough, it was poor Vandeleur who steered the conversation toward eternal life. Cloudsley had been asking after the political climate in Jamaica in the wake of the war; specifically, whether or not granting self-governance to the Maroons had eased some of the difficulties experienced by sugar planters.

"Yes, somewhat," said Vandeleur, puffing on his cigar. "They are a difficult people to trust, of course. I am not so foolish as some of my fellow planters, who think all rebellion has been civilized out of them. They still have their witches who practice obeah." He said the word in a quieter voice, as if he did not wish to be overheard.

"Surely you don't really believe in *obeah*," said another gentleman at the table.

"But I have seen evidence of it more than once."

"Really?" said the Count of St. Germain, leaning forward. "Do tell us more, Mr. Welby? I, for one, would be fascinated to hear what you have to say on the matter."

Vandeleur took a long swallow of port wine. "Some things do not bear repeating, especially when in such pleasant company. But you can mark my words, obeah is real, and powerful enough to keep the dead from their reward."

"And to keep the living from dying at all," added Chidike, as he refilled his master's cup.

"Surely you don't mean these sorcerers have discovered the secret of eternal life," said Dionysios, entering the conversation for the first time.

Vandeleur shrugged and ground out the stub of his cigar in an ashtray. "That I cannot say. What about you, St. Germain? Aren't *you* immortal? However do you manage it? Fell magics? Alchemical mastery? Clean living and piety?"

"I have never claimed to be immortal," said the Count, in his amiable way. "Just that I have had a good, long life, and hope to have a few more years in the world before I meet my maker." St. Germain was not smoking, and drank only barley water. "It is more interesting, I think, to contemplate what our new friend Dionysios has said. What do we all think? What sort of immortality would you choose? Metaphorical or actual? Let us have a conversation about *that*. Would you rather live forever through memory—have your deeds spoken of and your name remembered for all time—or would you rather live forever, forsaking your friends and lovers many times over, eventually keeping to the shadows and the sidelines of society for fear of persecution?"

The debate was a pleasant one. Everyone else found it an interesting conundrum, so I was happy to sit back and watch—until Dionysios, noting my silence, leaned across the table.

"Mr. Bretwynde, I have not heard your perspective. What do you think?"

"I have no opinion either way. As to the first option, I have never done anything that anyone would ever consider memorializing. As for the second—he did not specify one would live on in good health. I must daily endure the symptoms of a physical affliction that cannot be treated by any medicine, modern or ancient. The notion of enduring *that* for more than sixty years is unpleasant to me, much less six hundred."

"I did not know," said Dionysios. "I am sorry to hear it."

"What about you?"

"The second, of course," he said without hesitation. "I already live in obscurity; I am a servant. But with enough lifetimes under my belt, I might make something more of myself. To be young forever—I know you will think me lacking any sensibility, but that seems worth a few friends and lovers. I have already gained and lost many companions during my life, and known so few unique individuals, that I cannot help but think the opportunity to do so perpetually would justify attending the occasional funeral. Then again—why, Mr. Bretwynde, I think I've upset you. I'm very sorry. It was not my intention to do so."

The young man had indeed disturbed me with his callous speech, but I did not wish to say so. "I was merely going to say that the Count's proposal did not specify eternal youth—merely immortality. Would you say the same to everything, the funerals, losing friends, if you remained alive, but a rickety old man with no hair on his head but plenty in his ears, unable to woo a woman or read a book for want of sharper eyes?"

Dionysios giggled, one of the blithest sounds I have ever heard. For some reason I could not at that time fathom, it pleased me to see him relax and joke with me. "Perhaps not," he admitted. "That is what I would get for trusting the devil, wouldn't I?"

"Now now, who said anything about the devil?"

A momentary hush had fallen over the company, so when I said "devil," all turned to look at us. I blushed; Dionysios opened his mouth to respond, but just then a footman appeared, and with him was a tall, strikingly handsome, mustached man.

"Mr. Absalom Bernard," announced the flunky.

I stood to greet him, but not so quickly as Dionysios.

"Sir, allow me to get you a cup of wine," he said, heading to the sideboard.

I was amazed—amazed, and saddened. His affect had completely, totally changed in mere moments. Gone was the humor from his sweet mouth; the sparkle from his eye. All that remained was perfect servitude.

"I see you have been enjoying yourself in my absence," said Mr. Bernard to Dionysios. "Well, well. When the cat's away, as they say. Good evening, Mr. Bretwynde. Please, forgive my lateness. I was kept from pleasure by pressing business—but the night is a fine one, and still young, though it is already dark."

***

Upon my word, I have gotten off track with this last bit. Ah well; a little disorganization shan't confuse me, I don't think, when I am old and grey, and reading this to recall what time has erased from my mind. Flipping back through what I have written, I see I was intending to unveil how I discovered the second part of Jessamine's letter. Back to that, then.

In my unhappiness, I had thrown the offending letter down upon the Turkish kilim that graces my father's study, vowing to never look upon it again. (I was, at that point, merely making enquiries—not resolved as I am now, to create this chronicle.) It was wholly repellant to me, the contents of her missive—not only due to my jealousy but also the news regarding dear Phylotha, who was, it seemed, far worse off than I had ever imagined. I had, of course, seen her after—

No, I will keep to my point. I will come to all of that in time.

So here is what happened: there lay Jessamine's letter on the floor, crumpled from where I had gripped the edges in my grief. I snatched up the pile, thinking to throw the entirety of her communication into the fire. But clutching the envelope I realized it felt too heavy to be empty. Unfolding it a second time, I saw several pages I had not noticed, written in a far hastier script than the initial missive. Jessamine, it seemed, had written a second letter!

> Julian,
> My conscience troubles me, having told a falsehood when I wrote that I had "told you all" about that

night. Indeed, that is not the case. I spent more time with Denys than I initially confessed. When I closed my first letter, I was reluctant to recount the whole story. My hesitancy was out of concern for Denys, given the personal nature of our final encounter. After thinking more upon the matter, I believe telling you everything will do more to clear his name of any wrongdoing than keeping quiet would.

Where I had left off, my sister was escorting me to my rooms. Usually, when Mother is displeased by my behavior, she gives instructions to have me locked in, but Phylotha did not say anything about it that night. Perhaps she had seen how dispirited I had become after my initial outburst, for instead of further admonitions, she helped me undress and sat down on the bed to brush my hair.

"Sister," she said, "you may think me harsh when I correct your conduct, but please understand I do so only because I love you."

She could not know my unhappiness was the result of my verbal rumbullion with dear Denys, not her harangue. But I refused to speak to her of it, being, understandably, somewhat cross with her. After giving me a chance to respond, and finding me unwilling, Phylotha continued.

"Jess, I wouldn't be surprised if you had already discerned this, but the difference in our ages is because you were, well, a *surprise*, let us say. Not an unpleasant surprise—you know our parents have oft spoken about how they wanted more children, as well as an heir. But as much as Father wished Mother had been more fecund, for the seven years before you arrived I spent equal time wishing for a sister! When you came along, I was overjoyed...yet I know that the difference in our ages has made friendship difficult. Why, I was half-grown when you were a babe! How could we know true sisterly sympathy, with such a monumental gulf between us?

"So please understand that I chide you because, as a young girl, I made so many...let us call them *mistakes*, due to my high spirits, having received less parental observation than you have enjoyed. They learned better after me, you see. Surely you do not think I *chose* to wait until I was twenty to marry?"

I sighed then, for marriage is the absolute most boring of topics to me!

I could hear the smile in Phylotha's voice. "I know matrimony does not concern you now, but as I said in the parlor, it will. Your inheritance, while more than many young women will receive, is not enough to attract the right sort of suitors if you do not receive an offer before your youth has fled. I did not mean to be grim about my prospects; I know Julian would never object to your living here, once he and I are wed, but you may one day wish to be mistress of your own home. And if I have inherited our mother's difficulty conceiving, Tarrington may pass to someone disinclined to let you remain indefinitely. I know that is long, long in the future, but life is uncertainty, for women.

"I do not caution you because I agree with the way things are—I caution you because I fear for your future. Julian is a dear, but three years my junior, and not in the best of health. I like him very much, but neither of us have ever shied away from acknowledging mutual need as well as mutual affection comprise the foundation of our eventual union."

"You don't love him?"

"Of course I love him," Phylotha assured me. "There are, after all, many kinds of love a woman may feel for a man. And speaking of, I am wanted below. Just—promise me you will think on what I have said, Jess? Please?"

I promised her, mumbling the words, for I was still vexed—with her, with how my night had gone. Looking sad and a bit wistful, Phylotha embraced me, and departed.

Oh Phylotha! Had I known that would be our last conversation, how differently I should have comported myself! I would have said much to you—how I was sorry to be such a willful, difficult child, how I appreciated your guidance even if I rebelled against it—how I, too, had regretted the distance between us produced by the unfortunate difference in our ages. I would have returned your embrace instead of pulling away. I only hope that if you remember me, it is fondly, and with forgiveness...

Some time after my sister left me I feel asleep on the couch in my room. I had not gone to bed, for the ruckus coming from the gardens was very loud, though when I looked out my window I could see nothing of what might be transpiring. I was of course curious to know what the shrieks of laughter and bursts of song were all about, but I knew should I sneak out there and be caught I would be severely punished—and, having found a copy of *The Fortunes and Misfortunes of the Famous Moll Flanders* on a bookshelf in your house, I was nothing loath to stay in and read as much as I could before I was inevitably forced to relinquish the volume, my mother having forbidden me to read it.

It was past two when I startled awake, not completely certain where I was, or why. Then I heard someone calling my name softly, and a second knock. I nearly fell off the couch when I went to answer this strange nocturnal summons, so badly had my legs cramped, but I hobbled over and opened the door to find, of all people, Denys.

"Let me in," he said. "I should not be discovered here, speaking to you at this hour."

"All right," I said, having already forgotten Phylotha's earlier warnings. "Come in, then."

"I have awoken you…forgive me, there was a light in your window. I had to speak to you before I left," he said, as he carefully shut the door behind him. "I did not think I would get another chance."

"I am surprised you wanted one."

"I apologize," he said with a bow. "I was angry, and spoke rashly. But I would have us remember one another as friends. Can you forgive me?"

"Only if you will forgive me first," I replied.

"Of course," he assured me, and then very nearly swooned. "I'm sorry," he gasped, "may I sit?"

Only then did I notice the state of my friend. Where earlier in the evening he had been beautifully groomed, his clothing pressed and perfect, some terrible event had clearly befallen him. His wig was askew, and I could see the dark chestnut of his hair peeking out; his coat was rumpled, and several buttons were missing from his waistcoat.

"My God," I exclaimed, pushing him down onto the settee. "Sit! Please, be at ease! What on earth has happened to you?"

"Nothing," he said, and I heard the weariness in his voice. "I just wish to rest here with you for a few minutes before I am missed. Your company will soothe me more than recounting my troubles."

"All right," I said, though I was not a little curious. "I wish I could offer you something more than water, but if I ring, there will be trouble."

"I have had enough wine." He sighed. "Jess, I am sorry. I know how difficult and restrictive the world is for young ladies, even ones so wealthy as yourself… but please know that being a boy doesn't necessarily mean life is easy, especially when you are in service."

"I know more than a little about obedience, of course," I said, "but I am able to escape it without similar repercussions as you must fear. If I run from my duty to read a book, or play a game, or do nothing at all, I may be beaten or slapped or sent to my room without supper, but unless I do something truly terrible I need never fear being turned out into the street." I giggled. "Though come to think of it, being caught with a boy in my rooms at this hour in the morning might do it."

"I shall hide if someone draws near," he promised. "But yes, I think we both have much to complain of—and there is no need to fruitlessly compare ourselves to see who is the worse off." He shook his head. "I truly regret—well, I have many regrets. But mostly, I regret the necessary brevity of our friendship. I hope you will remember me after tonight. I know I will remember you."

"You speak as if I will never see you again," I said. "Surely when the Bretwyndes have another party you will attend, will you not?"

My hands were clasped in my lap as we sat together, and he patted them kindly. "I think not," he said. "We—my master and I—will soon be quitting England, likely never to return, or at least, not for a long time. But the real truth of the matter is that we were not invited."

"Not invited by whom?"

"By anyone."

I was a little shocked. I had never heard of such a thing in my life! It seemed absurd to me; who attends a party where none are of their acquaintance? Parties are boring even when you know everyone! I said as much, and Dionysios laughed.

"You are right—though I protest one small point: this party, though I knew no one, was hardly boring. But I agree, in a general sense. Truly, my master and I had reasons other than company for coming here."

I recalled our earlier conversation. "You wished to meet the Count of St. Germain," I said slowly.

Denys nodded. "And…"

"And what?"

He sighed. "Regrettably, certain circumstances have compelled my master to desire an earlier departure than he initially intended. It is a shame…the Count does seem to possess some remarkably strange abilities. Though I must confess, having met him, I do not believe he is all he says he is. Like everyone else, I suppose."

"What were you expecting?" Denys seemed so troubled. "Did you really believe he was two thousand years old?"

Denys shrugged. "It is difficult for me to say what I believed. *Hoped*, perhaps, would be a better word."

"Why?"

He looked at me so queerly. I shivered.

"Do you not wish to be young forever?"

"No!" The notion did not appeal to me at all. What Phylotha had said, about always being a child in my parents' house, it finally made sense to me. To be always under their control, subject to their authority? How repellant! "I have many reasons for wishing to grow up."

"Growing up only means growing *old*," said Denys, studying the back of his hand, then turning it over to observe his fingernails. "You cannot avoid it; they are the same thing. Age is…it is like mold, the way it grows and grows and finally covers everything; appearing suddenly in one spot, it seems trifling, but before you know it, all is ruined."

"That is rather bleak."

"But not untrue."

I shrugged. "Nothing can stop one growing older."

"No?" Again, that queer look in his eyes! "There are, in fact, many ways to prevent it—if the alchemists and the Chinese philosophers and men like the Count are to be believed."

"Are they, though? To be believed, I mean?"

"Yes," he said, with such certainty I dared not

disagree. "I myself have seen—"

But before he could say what he had seen, a blood-curdling scream pierced the night. We both rushed to the window. Though we saw burning torches illuminating many parts of the grounds, including the pleasure-garden and the hedge maze, we could spy nothing but the occasional dark shape running hither and yon. I had no concern in that moment that it might have been Phylotha, but I wonder now...

Another scream cut through our reverie. It startled Denys and he headed for the door.

"I must go," he said, "I have tarried here too long. I am wanted—needed—elsewhere. I shouldn't have come at all." His eyes were wide like a frightened horse's. I could see his nostrils flaring with each breath he drew, and he seemed pulled toward the doorway, as if some force drew him towards it. "Jess, you must forgive me—"

"You have your duties," I said, taking his hand and leading him towards the door. "Go. But remember what you said."

"What did I say?" He was clearly distracted, eager to be gone.

"That you would remember me."

His eyes focused on me once again, and I feared I had offended him; he looked like he might cry.

"I will *never* forget you," he said, "not as long as I live."

"Even if you live forever?"

He smiled. "*Especially* if I live forever."

And then he was gone. I shut the door behind

him and returned to the window, hoping to catch a final sight of him. A few moments later a slender figure darted out from the house and into a circle of torchlight just beyond the first hedge of the pleasure-garden. It was Denys. He paused, turned, and looked up at where I stood. I could feel his eyes on me. He waved at me, and ran. Where he went from there I do not know.

Now I have told you all I know, all that happened. As you can see, nothing untoward passed between us; quite the contrary.

Julian, I tell you truly, though he and I spent less than five hours in one another's company, I felt more of a connection with him than many friends with whom I have spent entire seasons. I hope he does succeed on his quest for immortality, though I do not understand it. Perhaps I never will.

I have puzzled over every word he spoke since almost the very moment we parted, but have found no answers for the question of why anyone should be so horrified by the prospect of growing older. I feel I have much to look forward to. Even if life truly is uncertainty for women, as Phylotha said, well, uncertainty is rarely boring. And the older a woman gets, the less rules she need follow. Just look at Lady Nerissa...

Yours always,

Jess

I was much calmer when I reached the conclusion of this second of Jessamine's letters. Though intriguing, nothing it contained much surprised me—much.[3] It did not surprise me that Dionysios had been so bold as to visit her in her chambers. And I already knew of his troubles in the garden that had left him rumpled prior to his calling on Jessamine for a final time. That I shall come to presently, for Cloudsley was the next of my correspondents.

No, it was Jessamine's final, rhetorical questions regarding Dionysios' obsession with eternal youth that struck me more than anything else in her letter. She is right, of course, how odd it was that such a young man should be so worried about his own aging. I, too, was intrigued by this part of him; he had spoken to me about it, at length. When I told him I did not fear death, he replied he feared nothing at all—he simply did not wish to die. This, of course, was after our conversation over port wine and cigars, much later in the night. Later even, I believe, than his conversation with Jessamine.

***

As I begin to record Cloudsley's letter, it occurs to me that I have no idea if I have deviated once again from the matter at hand.

---

3. I am certain if Jessamine knew how much pain she would cause me by repeating my former fiancée's sentiments regarding our being "mutually aware" of our "mutual need" for matrimony, she would not have included the remark. Phylotha's assurances surely gave her sister confidence her disclosure would not shock me. And yet, it did shock me, to hear myself called a "dear" and that she "liked me very much." As I write this, the sting has faded as completely as my engagement to Phylotha, but at the time, I felt like a little boy who had childishly proposed marriage to a much older woman, and been patted on the head for it. Ah, well. Upon further perusal, I wonder just how deep my dear Phylotha's deception went...her reference to youthful mistakes makes it seem as if she was counting on my "gratitude" over her returning my affections in more ways than one. But it is all in the past. It is difficult to remain angry with one who suffers so dreadfully, but at the same time, Jessamine's account has allowed me to regret the loss of our future together slightly less than I might have otherwise. –J.B.

This narrative was intended to be a record concerning the Count of St. Germain's visit. And it is…but, paging through what I have written, I find that the man himself has fallen in to a supporting rôle. I am not sure why that is. Perhaps it is because Jessamine was so unconcerned with him. So, I found, was Cloudsley, though that was less surprising. Cloudsley was never one to pay attention to a gentleman when a lady was about. Or at least, someone he believed to be a lady.

Cloudsley James was a school friend of mine; we both attended Wadham College, though he spent a greater amount of time there than I. To my supreme disappointment, I suffered a severe attack of my illness during my second year, compelling me to return home before completing my degree. I had every intention of returning, I loved Oxford…but as my father was forced to depart for Flanders not long after my homecoming, it was decided it would be better for me to remain at Tarrington. Cloudsley stayed on, but remembered me, and wrote to me often. Though he was more intrigued by the philosophical than the literary (the exact opposite of myself), his studies were still of great interest to me.

When he had completed his course he came and visited us before departing for a continental tour. Oh, how I longed to go with him! To wake up and see France, or Spain, or Italy outside my windows, instead of my own grounds; to tramp over ancient ruins and explore foreign forests instead of taking short turns about my gardens! Alas, such adventures have always been denied to me, being sickly by nature, and unable to tolerate much sun. But I think Cloudsley understood my frustration, and did his best to help by sending me frequent letters. I still keep them, though they contain fewer tidbits of historical or cultural interest than matters more interesting to Cloudsley. Here is a bit of one, from when he was traveling in the Ottoman Empire:

You can't imagine how warm the Aegean is! Upon my word, I have never found sea-bathing so delightful. One feels so refreshed, so invigorated, by a daily swim in salt waters, especially ones as salty as these. Yes, I do think these are the saltiest waters I have ever swum in. Interesting, eh? You should think about coming here to treat your whatever-you-have. Bath, though pleasant, is so small that one always feels as though they are on top of some weeping, peeling invalid; here, there is so much sea and sky and space I imagine it's possible to go for weeks without ever seeing another human—well, if one didn't need meals prepared, clothing washed, or desire female company, I suppose. That reminds me, the women here, Julian! I can't even tell you how delightful they are. And so eager to please! The stories I could tell! It is really too bad you could not come along; I've learned a thing or two from the girls here, which means they could teach you more than quite a lot. I tell you what, I will bring you a harem girl if I can find one for sale. I have heard they are valued by how many nutmegs one can press into their navels. Well, I care nothing for navels, not being a Turk, so perhaps I can find one to be had for cheap due to a tragically small umbilicus. I say, they are beautiful, with eyes that contain all the stars in the heaven and simply enormous milk-paps riper and firmer even than a honeymelon.

Quintessential Cloudsley. I use this passage as an exemplar as it shows exactly how he was. I am sorry to say he has changed, and like myself, not for the better.

There were several things I wished to ask Cloudsley. Aware even as I wrote the words of how the focus of my inquiry had broadened and shifted, I sent to him a letter asking the following questions, in the hopes of further satisfying my curiosity:

1. Whether Cloudsley had invited Mr. Absalom Bernard to Tarrington (While Dionysios told Jessamine that he and his master were not invited, he had told me that the Lady Nerissa invited Mr. Bernard—and Lady Nerissa heard that Cloudsley had invited them)

2. What he remembered of the wager between Mr. Absalom Bernard and poor Vandeleur (It bothered me that, concerning Chidike's alleged murder of Vandeleur, Mrs. Welby believed that Chidike was wagered, and thus sought revenge; I recalled a different wager, and hoped Cloudsley's recollections would allow me to present some evidence in defense of Chidike, as I had still found none beyond my own memory)

3. If he had proposed marriage to the girl he met and fell in love with during the Count's visit (I never heard the end of his…let us call it a *scheme*, given the general uproar caused by Phylotha's fit)

4. What he could possibly mean by demanding the Tydfils pay him five hundred pounds what with their daughter in such a state (I mean, *really*)

All this I put into a letter. Two days later a rather waspish reply came to me from the magistrate of Chittlehampton, asking if I would be so good as to promptly write, or come meet with him, as they had need of Chidike's cell, and would like it vacated one way or the other. If I had evidence, I should present it at once, for the case seemed decided.

I felt so very guilty over my inability to travel and help Chidike I wept and raged over my condition, and over the situation itself. I resolved that if three days hence I had not heard from Cloudsley, I would muster myself and go to Vandeleur's former servant.

Not being trained in the law, I had no knowledge if my assertion Chidike had not been wagered could save him, but I felt it was my duty to try.

But all this planning was for naught. The following morning I received an answer from Cloudsley. It troubled me greatly.

I am amazed you would send me such a cheeky, insensitive letter, but due to our long friendship I shall give you the benefit of the doubt and assume you do not know the whole of my troubles.

No, I did not invite Mr. Bernard to your home. However did you come up with such a wild notion? I had never met him or his niece before that night; surely that much was obvious, even to you? Are you trying to be funny? Perhaps you were. I've always said you had no talent for humor.

I suspect you are having another jape at my expense by asking whether I proposed to the youthful goddess who yet torments my heart, for you must know very well that I did not. Likely you think that amusing, as I'm sure you still believe, in spite of her bewitching, feminine wiles that "Dionysios" was a boy. Well, go on then, laugh at me! Laugh at this tormented, shattered ruin of a man, if you so desire. I never thought you cruel, Julian, but you must have a nasty streak somewhere to mock me in my agonies. Especially as all of this pain I endure is, if not the result of your actions, a result of your invitation.

I am not exaggerating when I call myself tormented, ruined. *That*, since you asked, is why I am requiring the sum of five hundred pounds be paid to me by the Mallorys. Phylotha, that mad bitch, not only robbed me of any future happiness with the only girl I ever wanted to take to wife, but also the entirety of my former vigor. Upon my word, the tone of your letter, asking me what I meant by asking for modest restitution and whether I am aware of her "situation!" I am perhaps more aware of her situation than anyone else, and thus know I am being reasonable. If your former fiancée prospered, I would ask for quite a bit more, to console me in the forced isolation I must now endure for I know not how much longer. But, as the gods have seen fit to punish her for her behavior, I ask only the bare minimum.

Lest you think me callous, let me explain in slightly more detail. Come to think of it, while I'm at it, I'll go one step further, and provide you with the evidence regarding the aforementioned female-in-question's female-ness so you will stop mocking me.

As you know, Dionysios—I never did ascertain the girl's real name—attracted my attention when first I saw her serving wine at dinner that night. She was a vision, even dressed as a pageboy. Those lips, those eyes; her eyebrows, her finely sculpted cheekbones, she was like Venus herself—nay, like Artemis, for no seductive archness marred her perfect, virginal countenance. To be fully honest, seeing her dressed as a boy inflamed me all the more, for I saw how slender, how well-turned were her ankles and calves, and in equal measure the strength and softness of her thighs. I was free to admire her figure even more than I would have been had she sat at table with us, like that rat-faced younger sister of Phylotha's who kept shooting me the dirtiest looks all throughout the meal. The sight of that awful creature furrowing her hedgerow of a brow at me very nearly gave me indigestion. I have long been convinced Jessamine is not only a tribade-in-training but also a witch; I wonder if she didn't curse me. At any rate, she futilely tried to stop my attentions to Dionysios by crying out *"leave that boy alone!"* before her mother hushed her up, but I would not leave off. The chit had either not discerned Dionysios' secret, or was trying to throw me off the scent so she could have her for her own. I wondered the same about you, too, the latter I mean, after that tiresome lecture you gave me *in re* my behavior toward guests in your home, but it became obvious enough you thought I was making overtures toward a boy. Had I been younger I shouldn't have been so offended, but I have not done such a thing since Wadham; a man grows out of his childish infatuations with the same sex—well, most of us do, Julian. Ha ha. You see, I too can make jokes at another's expense.

Honestly, though, I do not blame you for reprimanding me, even if it was unnecessary. I, too, might have felt compelled to take a strong tone with a friend if I, in a similar state of ignorance, had seen what you saw. But you must understand, I warmed the girl's cockles considerably by pulling her onto my lap and letting her feel just how well I could wriggle and pump. All that fussing when she spilled the wine on the Count of St. Germain was just an excess of excited sensations on her part—and dismay over displaying a chink in the armor, of course, for she was acting a part. Think on it, a real servant could have taken twice what I gave her without spilling a drop. But you saw her blushing, did you not? That is a sign, of course, of feminine arousal. As you may or may not know. Ha ha!

Truly, the girl was *infatuated* with me. I know you won't believe me, as you likely perceived how she kept her distance after the incident at dinner, but that was all due to her knowing her money-hungry uncle would soon be arriving to work his schemes. And that was, I admit, all for the best. When her uncle called her to the cards-table after Jessamine's amusing outburst and subsequent banishment (that is the wages of sin right there), I was done for. I could not focus on the game for desiring her, and so gave over quickly.

Not so with Vandeleur, as I'm sure you recall. I do not mean he also desired Dionysios; no, he was more interested in betting, even though Mr. Bernard had already demonstrated several times over that was better than the devil himself at cards. It was awful, was it not, watching your cousin wager away nearly everything he owned? But I do not feel at all responsible, for I'm sure you recall how he would not listen to any of our attempts to dissuade him. Ah—yes, as to whether Chidike was ever at stake, I cannot recall. I *do* remember Mr. Bernard putting his niece upon the auction block, but that was merely an alternative means toward their mutual end, as I intuited at the time. I feel you rolling your eyes, Julian—I feel it through time and through space—but give it some more consideration. Of what was Vandeleur speaking, just before those final, fateful hands? The delicacy of his wife's situation, of course! He practically said that he expected her to expire in the course of giving birth to his latest offspring. Thus, *of course* that blackguard Mr. Bernard put up his niece. If he won the hand, he would have the plantation. If he lost, his niece would be well-placed in Vandeleur's service, to seduce him. You know, like in *Twelfth Night!* It makes perfect sense.

But of course Mr. Bernard won his hand, and Vandeleur became so incensed the Count felt compelled to intercede. You may recall Vandeleur did not wish to be diverted, and carried on quite a bit before Dionysios, that angel, interrupted, volunteering herself as an assistant to whatever *fête* the Count had in mind. I have no notion of whether she was eager to see some magic done, or anxious to turn the conversation away from the violence Vandeleur all but promised he would do to her uncle, but her manners were charming either way.

Though it disappointed Dionysios, I wasn't at all sorry when the Count turned down that dear creature and instead insisted Vandeleur assist him. I reckoned if the girl was unattached, it would be easier to catch her alone and make her fully aware of my intentions toward her. And so it was. All eyes were upon the Count as he announced his "uncontrollable urge to perform a sacred rite passed down to modern man from the ancient world." During all the commotion caused by his declaration I was able to sneak several pinches and a few caresses of the girl's pert little bottom before her uncle noticed and herded her away from me. I mention this as no boy's bottom was ever so perfect as the one I sensed beneath her trousers. No, when I felt those glorious cheeks in my hand, it was like an aperitif of lust. My God, but she set me on fire; I knew I must have her before the night was out, or die.

It was with the utmost impatience that I followed the herd out to the pleasure-gardens; I was restless to the point of distraction as St. Germain commanded torches be lit and supervised the servants in setting up the altar with bowls, candles, a silver dagger, all that nonsense. Indeed, as everyone but myself seemed positively enthralled by the hoopla, I took the opportunity to wander close to Dionysios whilst the Count wove grape leaves into a crown and braided ivy-leaves around some old walking-stick.

Her uncle sensed what I was about and drew her in front of him. You, who have insisted she was a boy, and a servant, should take some time to think about why exactly Bernard would have put his hand on a servant's shoulder and squeezed it, then favored her with a sparkling, warm, avuncular smile as the "magic show" progressed? *Hmm?* Surely even a favored pageboy would warrant only a pat on the head. No no, their interactions were that of an old uncle thrilled to see his niece's enthusiasm for a bit of mummery, or I'm no judge of character at all.

You see, I am building my case for Dionysios' femininity as I get to why exactly I require financial restitution from your former fiancée's family!

If I am recalling correctly, you, for once, weren't doing that insufferable thing you do when you're playing host, where you flit from person to person, wringing your hands and asking everyone if they're having a good enough time, and when they tell you yes, trying to make it even better in ways they don't want. No; you were absolutely enthralled by the unfolding chicanery. Perhaps if you'd been paying a little more attention to your fiancée, none of us would be in this pickle. But alas, your eyes were saucers as the Count helped the much-embarrassed Vandeleur up onto a cloth-draped trunk, where he was forced to mimic the posture of that ghastly statue of Bacchus you have in the center of your garden, goblet of wine in one hand and staff in his other, with a crown of leaves on his head.

You know, I've never seen anything so queer in all my life. For some reason I've always found that statue to be a little unsettling, even by daylight—but under the crescent moon, with the torches sputtering and the night-birds hooting, I tell you Julian, it really gave me a turn. I know I'm only giving you more fodder for mocking me, but really, the statue seemed to be looking down at Vandeleur. Its expression seemed different. I've always felt the sculptor gave that Bacchus an expression more mischievous than jovial, but that night, he looked wicked. Sinister. It may have been only the shadows, but then again, given what happened...

Ah, perhaps it was simply the oddness of St. Germain's proceedings that altered my perceptions. You noticed nothing different about the statue, I'm sure; your eyes were on the Count when he took a candle from the altar and ignited a bowl of vegetation, muttering an incantation that may have been Greek.

Given his terrible accent, I'm not entirely sure.

Your fiancée was by your side, as is proper, right at the front, and I saw her get a face full of smoke when the wind shifted and the leaves flared dramatically against the night. *That* was what caused her to cry out and collapse, if you didn't notice. I wonder at you, Julian; that you stood on dumbly while Phylotha's mother and some other women caught her before she fell to the ground, and sought to revive her by fanning her face. You really are a disgrace. Your mother, who was clearly more concerned for your then-fiancée's health, rushed to Vandeleur and snatched his glass of wine to try to revive her. Thank goodness it worked, and got Phylotha on her feet again, though when I saw the look in her eyes, I remember feeling rather repelled. She seemed *strange.* I suppose that's because she was. I believe St. Germain knew something had gone awry, as well, for I remember him looking keenly at the girl before returning the cup to your cousin.

After that, to your credit, you did your manly duty and escorted Phylotha back into the house. Sadly for you, that was when things really got interesting. A few more hand-wavings and mutterings, and the Count began to speak, carrying on with his diversion as though nothing at all had happened.

"Now, Mr. Welby," he said, "are you ready to 'take on the god,' as they said in ancient Greece?"

"I suppose," said Vandeleur, clearly unhappy to be standing there with a sheet draped and pinned over his dinner clothes. "Do get on with it."

"Patience, young man," said St. Germain. "One

does not hastily summon a deity—at least, it is never wise to do so." Dipping his finger in the ashes of the burned ivy-leaves he dotted a rough outline of a cluster of grapes on Vandeleur's forehead, and bid him drink from his cup of wine. Then he began to chant.

"O Bacchus, wild god of the vines and creatures and of the trees," intoned the Count, "grace us with your presence this warm summer's night! Join us so we may know the freedom your godhead grants! *Euhoi! Euhoi!* Come, Bacchus!"

It's a shame you had gone off with Phylotha, given how interested you were in the proceedings, for the next bit was fascinating. Vandeleur stiffened, as if someone had applied a birch rod to his bottom, and his eyes got all wide like he was having a fit. He grimaced, his face contorting until he looked like a tragedian's mask, like someone else entirely, and cried *"Euhoi!"*

Everyone gasped, even myself. Even his voice had changed. It was very queer, to see Vandeleur go from bored and awkward to ecstatic.

"Welcome, Bacchus—Eleutherios—Oeneus! Many thanks for honoring us this night," said St. Germain. "You are most welcome."

"What would you ask of me?"

"Your humble worshipers," he gestured to his very still audience, "request a demonstration of your power."

"Do they not trust in such?"

"It isn't that," said the Count quickly. "But you know how Christians can be. They like to see miracles."

Vandeleur laughed and laughed at this blasphemy, merrier than I have ever seen him before. "Well then," he replied, "let us show them something they will understand, shall we?"

"We are of one mind, O Bacchus." The Count bowed, and, removing a bowl of some dark liquid from the altar, walked to the edge of the crowd, and bid your mother take a sip.

"Grape juice?" she asked.

"Grape juice," confirmed the Count. He returned to where Vandeleur posed beneath the statue. "Bacchus, bless this juice, oh you who squeezed the first grape! Turn it into wine!"

Vandeleur lowered his decorated shillelagh and dipped the tip into the bowl. To everyone's surprise—even the Count's, I think, given the way he jumped—a bright crimson light erupted from the bowl, and just as quickly disappeared.

St. Germain passed the bowl back to your mother, who sipped—and cried out.

"It *is* wine!" she exclaimed. "My God!"

"No, my lady," said Vandeleur, in that same, high but sonorous voice, so unlike his usual tone, "a different god entirely."

The small crowd erupted into murmurs, but there was no applause. As the bowl was passed from mouth to mouth so everyone could have a taste, your guests seemed divided on whether this was remarkable, sacrilegious, entertaining, or all three. I, for my part, didn't know what to think. Though at first I had seen this diversion as an annoyance, taking up time that I desired to use in another fashion, it had become really very interesting. And, I noted, glancing over at Dionysios, it was affecting that young lady considerably. Her eyes shone like the stars, and her rose-petal complexion was rosier than ever, I could tell even in the dim light. She was enchanted by everything, and I had hopes seeing such "magic" would soften her up to suggestions of another sort, later on.

"We thank you for your gift," said St. Germain, after placing the empty bowl upon the altar. "But I would show these people more. I ask of you that you turn our gathering into a true bacchanal," said the Count. A few indignant gasps from the ladies made the Count and Vandeleur smile. "And when I say bacchanal, I am asking that you bless us so we may drink wine and toast you, and dance, and sing songs, all to honor the great liberator! You will help us, will you not, O Bacchus?"

"I shall, but I require your help to do so." Vandeleur's matter-of-factness was odder than anything else. I found myself wondering if they had arranged this all beforehand—but when? Your cousin was too hot-tempered before reaching the gardens to listen to anyone, and I doubted St. Germain had asked him before the card-playing began. After all, Vandeleur had not acted like one "in on a joke" when the Count proposed this diversion, which was, of course, to divert Vandeleur from his rage over losing Nineveh to Mr. Bernard. Thus, his eagerly playing the part, so spontaneously after St. Germain called upon the ancient god…it was either black magic, or the most amazing set-up for a lark.

"Your servant awaits your instructions, O Bacchus,"

said the Count. "How may I assist you?"

"Let everyone have a cup of wine!"

St. Germain snapped his fingers, and servants hurried to fulfill the command. When everyone held an appropriate libation, Vandeleur, walking like one drunk, or perhaps half-asleep, wandered up to one of the many crones of your mother's acquaintance and kissed her on the forehead.

"Be a Bacchante, and know me better!" he cried.

Then, remarkably, the ancient baggage drained her cup, threw it away into the bushes, and bounded away in the direction of the hedge-maze nimbly as a deer, singing like a madwoman. Not a one of us had expected *that*. I glanced at St. Germain; even his eyes were wide, and his head was canted to the side, as if incredulous.

But Vandeleur had not paused; he repeated this with each woman, and then did the same for the few gentlemen (only he bid them know him as satyrs instead of nymphs), until only the Count, Mr. Bernard, myself, and Dionysios remained. I had, during the hubbub, edged behind a hedge to watch, as I must confess a bit of opportunism. I planned to escape the blessing, but chase after Dionysios after *she* had been blessed. Then, I felt certain I could make my move most effectively.

Vandeleur finally approached Mr. Bernard and his niece. Before the man could say a word, Mr. Bernard held up his hands, and said he meant no disrespect, but if it was all right with Bacchus, he preferred to further converse with St. Germain that night rather than drink and make merry. Vandeleur nodded sagely in acquiescence, and turned to Dionysios. But he paused, looking at her, and for the first time seemed uncertain.

"Would you receive my gift?" he asked. "Or would you have something else? There is much I would bestow upon you—you who, by your nature, are dear to my heart."

Dionysios, obviously startled, looked up at her uncle, who looked to the Count. The Count shrugged. Dionysios was left on her own.

"If you are truly a god, you know what I wish," she said softly. "Will you give it to me?"

Vandeleur laughed, a ringing, girlish laugh, unlike his usual oafish *hurr hurr.* The sound made my skin prickle.

"Oh, sweet child. You put me in such a quandary. You are one I would bless in all ways, grant whatever you desire...but what you want most, I cannot bestow. *That* is for the gods alone. There is another way, yes, but I do not think you are ready to journey to the Fortunate Isles...there is too much that binds you here, to this world. Is that not so, dear one?"

Dionysios' wide eyes were brimful of tears by the end of Vandeleur's odd speech; I saw them hovering there as she looked again to her uncle. It broke my heart, I tell you, to see her so distressed. I realized that she believed, *truly* believed, that Vandeleur had become a god for the evening, and had the power to change men with magic. At the time I thought her sweet and womanly for being so beguiled...but now, I cannot say what I believe.

At last Dionysios opened her perfect lips to speak,

but her voice broke, and only a raw, agonized cry of protest, or perhaps anger, came out. It hurt me, that sound that came from her throat, and inspired me in that moment to try to distract her from her grief. I was just about to bound out from behind my hiding place when you bumbled up.

"What did I miss?" I think is what you said, cheerfully, despite the expressions on everyone's faces.

"Please, you must excuse me," said Dionysios, raising her slender hand to her brow. "I am not feeling at all well. I will retire for the evening."

I saw it then, my opportunity. "Allow me to escort you," I said, emerging from my hiding-place.

"That's very kind of you, but—"

I took her by the arm. "I insist. You are in need, and with Mr. Bernard having already expressed a wish to converse with the Count, and Julian likely wanting to see to the needs of his guests, only I remain to assist you."

I saw your mind immediately go to those in the gardens; Mr. Bernard seemed more hesitant to release his niece into my company, but what could he do? To protest too strongly would give away Dionysios' secret, so he gave his consent.

"This way, my young friend," I said, guiding her to the house.

Oh, Julian, I tell you, in that moment my heart was pounding, my blood was up! I could have carried her the whole way, I felt so very invigorated. And she was pliant, responding to every direction like a well-trained horse. I cannot remember all I said to her, but as soon as we were out of earshot

I began to tell her of how I had discerned her true sex, and of my passion, my *love* for her, how she had taken possession of my heart the moment I saw her. I spoke of her beauty, her grace, her sweet sadness, everything I could think to say to win her affections.

Dionysios was quiet during my speech; a prettily mannered girl, she let me speak, only smiling and nodding when I paused for breath. It gave me hope that my words were not falling upon deaf ears—and yet, when we arrived at the door of your home, and I had exhausted most of what I had to say, I bowed her inside...at which point she turned 'round, and surprised me.

"I thank you for your compliments, Mr. James," she said quietly. "You are very kind, but I cannot return your affections. I regret the need to disappoint—"

"What's this? Can't return them? My girl, we both know you already do!"

"I beg your pardon?" She drew away from me, suddenly as cold as the marble her perfectly sculpted face so resembled. "You have grievously mistaken me, sir. Let us say no more about it—I am tired, and must rest. If you will excuse me, I will go and lie down."

Women, of course, are forced by society to parrot such platitudes for the sake of their reputation. As a modern-thinking, progressive sort of gentleman, I am keenly aware how regrettable it is that the weaker sex is mandated by convention to pretend to a lack of lubricity. Broad experience has taught me to see through this sort of feminine dissembling, however, and cut to the quick of their true feelings.

"Nonsense," I said, drawing her into a tight embrace before she could run off. "What you need is something that will awaken your vital spirits. I can help you with that. I guarantee that tomorrow you'll feel better—even if you are a bit sore."

"You are too forward." She struggled against me, wriggling her body as I held it close, further inflaming me. "Release me!"

"Dear creature, I shan't let you go until I've cured what ails you," I vowed, holding her fast with my left arm as with my right I untied her rose-colored cravat and set to work unbuttoning the waistcoat and loosening the shirt that hid her womanly charms from my view. She cried out, continuing to pretend at modesty, but I could no longer speak to reassure her, not after finally touching her skin! Yet just as I found a welcoming handful of something soft, like a fish she wriggled out of my grasp and fled up the stairs.

Oh, what a merry chase! Through the stairwells and hallways of Tarrington I followed her like a ferret after a hare. She ducked, but I weaved, always keeping her slender posterior in my sight. I have never run like that, not even the year I won the potato race at the Ivybridge village fair (I'm sure you remember), but local renown and half a crown were not as much of an inspiration, I suppose.

Still, she was a fleet-footed creature, and I was beginning to flag when at last she turned a corner too quickly and tripped on the edge of a runner. I fell upon her, victorious, so eager I was of a mind to satisfy my letch in front of a door rather than waiting to get behind one. But to my dismay, all the ruckus had disturbed the occupant of the room in question—and who should emerge but your former fiancée!

"I say," I said, getting to my feet. I offered Dionysios a hand up but she scooted away from me on all fours and then, gaining her feet, took off running down the hall, the tease. I told myself I would find her later; it seemed more gallant to attend to Phylotha, as she still did not appear wholly well. Her color was poor, and she was swaying on her feet. "Good evening, my dear. I'm sorry we awakened you. Can I help you back to your bed? Or are you feeling better?"

"Much," she replied. "I would love your help, however, if you would be so kind? I really must find him...quickly."

At the time I thought she meant you. Though I longed to seek Dionysios wherever she had secreted herself, likely someplace more comfortable for our lovemaking, I gave Phylotha my arm. A gentleman's duty and all that.

"All right," I said. "Let's go find him. I believe he's in the gardens. It should be easy enough to track him down."

"Do you really think so? He is so wild, elusive..."

"Oh, tosh." Still believing she spoke of you, I protested this description, understandably, you will admit. "Likely he's somewhere amongst the revelers. Elusive seems a bit over the top. I'm sure we'll find him easily enough."

"As you say," she murmured.

Silent, she walked with me back into the night air, though when the breeze tousled her hair she became more alert than I had seen her since before the start of St. Germain's ritual.

"He is close," she whispered.

"I'm sure," I said, leading her to the mouth of the hedge maze. "Let's go inside. I know the sequence."

As we walked through the lanes of the maze, the thick, enclosing vegetation black rather than green in the darkness of the night, I felt that same sense of uncertainty that I had felt watching St. Germain's earlier display. The breeze had kicked up, and every corner we turned it sounded more and more like the leaves were whispering to one another rather than rustling; every so often, in the distance, we heard bursts of discordant song, sometimes screaming or cheering, and once, the sounds of rutting. I was very curious indeed about who was having a go with whom among the biddies and scrawny gentlemen of your party. But when we turned a corner and Vandeleur came into view, lying casually beneath a tree in a small clearing, all other thoughts were chased from my mind, as it became suddenly very clear that *this* was who Phylotha truly sought.

"My lord!" she cried, and ran toward Vandeleur, falling at his feet in a heap and pressing her forehead to his knees. "It is truly you! Oh, I am so happy."

"My daughter, you have found me!" he said, sitting up and cradling her face in his hands, heedless of how awkward their bizarre intimacy must seem to me. "I was worried you would remain chained this night!"

Oh, how uncomfortable I was! I could not for the life of me discern if they were both mad, or had been carrying on some sort of affair under your nose. For your sake I would not leave them, though the screams and cries in the gardens were coming closer to where I was, and I dearly wanted to get back to Dionysios. The tragedy of it—had I known then what I know now, of course, I should have fled.

"I regret the loss of even a moment of your divine presence," she whimpered. "My lord, my god, my only master!"

I *ahem*ed into my fist to alert them to my presence.

"Steady on," I said, striding over to where they lay. "You've got this all wrong, Phylotha. *Julian* is your only master, or at least he will be soon enough. And you, Vandeleur, stop this nonsense immediately. The girl is clearly disturbed; don't further tax her wits. Come on, Phylotha. Up with you. Get off the ground, you're soiling your dress."

But it was Vandeleur who got to his feet, instead.

"Leave her be," he demanded, in that fruity, high, girlish voice. "She is an acolyte of a truer god than you will ever know! She should be commended for her devotion, not chastised."

"Come now," I protested. I was really angry at what I perceived as his callous indifference. "Drop this silly charade immediately. You can play your parlor games with the Count all you like when you have an audience, but it's just us now. Let's get her into bed. She's acting mad, can't you see that?"

"She *is* mad, or at least, so you would say," he replied, but helping her up all the same. "But I am not

Vandeleur, Mr. James. You know who I am; you saw me summoned, and take possession of this generous host. And yet, you refuse me honor?"

"I'll refuse you a lot more than that if you don't cease this freak!"

"Dear one, sweet one, child of my heart," he said unto Phylotha, "shall we show this unbeliever our true power? Do you think he needs a demonstration?"

"All must hear the clarion call of Eleutherios," she replied, her eyes focusing for the first time since her collapse.

Julian, I began to sweat. I sensed things were about to take a turn, but I had no idea, really, that she would attack me.

Vandeleur kissed her on the forehead, and then she *changed*. She bared her teeth at me, like a feral thing, like a mad dog, and then with a scream I'm sure they heard in the next county over she launched herself at me, hands outstretched, fingers clutching, foaming at the mouth.

I ran for it. I'm not proud of it, but what else could I do? Vandeleur was laughing like he'd just been told the funniest joke in the world, and Phylotha was yodeling, and everywhere around me I heard other, strange sounds. Yes, I bolted, and realized too late I had failed to count which ways I was turning. But I was panicking, I could hear her breathing and grunting like some fell beast of the wilderness.

God but she was fast, and unnaturally nimble. You know I have always been a champion tree-climber; in an attempt to get away from her I used a bench as a step up to grab the branch of a linden-tree when

I turned down a dead-end in the maze, and with a bit of effort, for the distance was not short, pulled myself up and over the hedge, and dropped down beside one of your mother's friends busily racking off what looked to be someone's valet. She was really going at it, her hand was moving at blinding speed, and she did not stop for a moment when I came crashing down practically on top of them. That was rather shocking, so imagine my surprise when I heard a cry, and saw Phylotha leap over the same partition without any assistance, and then land in a crouch beside them. Neither the woman nor the valet so much as looked up as Phylotha, snarling, rose up and, swaying, screamed again. Her wail was so loud I clapped my hands to my ears in terror, frozen in place.

That got the valet's attention; he was close to spending, I could tell, and was rather annoyed by all this ruckus.

"I say," he called at her, as your mother's friend continued to rapidly move her hand up and down his shaft. "Leave off with all that—if you're not going to help, then give us some privacy!"

It was a relief to me when Phylotha swung her head around to stare right at this fellow. He blanched, and rather comically given the situation, the hardest part of him went soft at the sight of her bewitched countenance. She was a frightful thing to behold, and I could see why he could not maintain in the face of all that.

"Hello," he said, as the lady attending him made little cooing sounds of disappointment and applied her mouth to try to revive his vigor.

I saw her lurch towards him, at which point I took off running yet again. I heard a scream, a male scream, and the laughter of two women before I was out of earshot.

I slowed my pace, thinking myself out of danger at last, but that was not the case. No, as I panted, leaning against the wall of the maze, I heard giggling, and then the two of them—Phylotha, and the woman who had been pleasuring the unfortunate man—turned the corner. I hoped for a moment that whatever they had done to that poor fellow had sated Phylotha's blood-lust, but when they saw me, they both assumed that same, crazed expression, and I did not linger to see what would happen if they caught me.

I cannot say how long that second chase lasted. I ran until my legs felt made of jelly, until the muscles of my arms burned like a fire every time I used them to assist me in my retreat.

Then, at last, I saw what I had hoped for: the exit of your infernal maze. Phylotha had left her companion behind, still after me like a hellhound, but I thought—hoped—that without hedges, well, hedging me in, perhaps I had a better chance of escaping her. I willed my legs to move, and like a horse who sees the finish line, I put on a burst of speed—only to run straight into Dionysios!

I completely bowled her over in my haste, had her on her back for the second time, though just as unable to take advantage of the situation.

"My love!" I gasped. "You must run, we must go! She's almost here, she's—"

"Euhoi! Euhoi!" cried someone from above me. I looked up to see Vandeleur there, waving Phylotha over to where I lay. I knew then I was done for, and kissed Dionysios on the mouth, one last sweet taste of the world before I arrived in heaven. Then I let her wriggle out from underneath me, hoping she could escape, but for all my concern, she simply bowed to Phylotha, and stranger still, Phylotha to her, before Dionysios bolted into the maze. It was the last time I saw her...

With a cold, cruel smile, your former fiancée sauntered over to me. I could smell her sweat and perfume as she knelt by my side, and grabbed the lapels of my jacket.

"Euhoi," she whispered—and bit me on the ear. I felt her teeth in my flesh, I felt blood running down my neck as I offered up my final prayer...but then I heard a cry of protest and opened my eyes to see St. Germain and Mr. Bernard standing over me, restraining the struggling Phylotha as Vandeleur collapsed into giggles on the ground.

"Run!" cried St. Germain.

I didn't wait to be told a second time.

You must apply to either Mr. Bernard or that creepy Count to find out what happened after that. As you know, I departed that very night, first visiting a local physician whom I managed to awaken and galloping home after he stitched me up. I had to shoot my horse; he was so exhausted he was foaming blood from his mouth by the time I arrived.

I loved that horse, but that is not the worst of it. No, Julian, the worst is that since that night, I dream of her. Your fiancée, I mean. I dream of the scent of her breath, the feel of her teeth, the smell of her. I see her wild rolling eyes every night. Thinking a good hard fuck with a normal woman would help I went into town a few nights back, in order to obtain that very thing, but that pleasure is denied me now too. I picked the finest of the pride at the establishment, but when she lifted up her skirts I began to scream, unable to stop myself from remembering Phylotha's legs beneath her torn dress. The girl tried to calm me by kissing me, but I flung her away from me and was forcibly ejected by a large man, face-first, into the street.

Now, I ask you, does five hundred pounds for a lost horse and a lost life seem so very cruel? Don't bother answering me. I cannot bear the thought of having more to do with you or yours.

Good luck to you Julian. Lord knows we all need it in this world.

—Cloudsley

***

Cloudsley's letter—the information it contained, the sentiments expressed in his closing—shocked me. I was speechless; nay, *powerless* upon finishing, and sat limply staring at it for some time in my study, as the afternoon light waned and distant thunder began to promise a dreary evening.

My former (apparently) friend was correct in his assumption that I had not heard the whole of what transpired during the time between when I put Phylotha to bed and hearing, much later in the night, that she had been apprehended, bloodied and insane, and locked in a closet for fear of her injuring additional guests. And yet, Cloudsley's account was so very outlandish it left me perplexed as to whether I could rely upon his sanity.

Cloudsley, despite all of what I must call his "notions," could never be described as *fanciful*. Additionally, he simply despised the classics, and especially Greek tragedy; I still recall allowing him to use my notes our first year at Wadham to study for an exam on Sophocles. Thus, my first conclusion—that Cloudsley was leading me on, claiming to have had some sort of modern experience of *The Bacchae*—felt wrong, the more I thought on it. No, it just didn't seem like him, not at all. While he had always been a practical joker, Cloudsley's larks always favored the sophomoric rather than the esoteric. Salting your wine when you looked away, tucking a guinea pig between your sheets before bedtime, shooting off a firework during a formal dinner…all that and more I would believe Cloudsley capable of, but not this sort of extensive, literary deception.

Which left only one conclusion: that something at least *similar* to what Cloudsley described had gone on during the night of the Count of St. Germain's concert. That is not to say I believed that the Count had actually summoned a god. Drugged wine would explain any eccentric or lewd conduct on behalf of my guests, for example. And as for Vandeleur, well, Cloudsley himself had suggested that he might have had a prior arrangement with St. Germain. That seemed most likely—after all, the Count *had* hastily suggested the diversion when Vandeleur became agitated, and Vandeleur, though so angry he was threatening Mr. Bernard with violence, had consented. Also, the Count had denied Dionysios the privilege of being his volunteer, though the boy, of the two of them, seemed more amenable to high jinks. The juice-into-wine routine could have been a mere mummer's trick. All this, taken together, could very well simulate some sort of genuine *bakkheia*. And as for Phylotha herself, if under the power of smoke and drugged wine she had indeed committed those vicious acts, she may have gone mad in the wake of realizing just what she had done.

Fortunately (if such a word may be used in any way as regards that fateful night) Cloudsley didn't perfectly reprise the *rôle* of Pentheus in *The Bacchae*. And yet, his description of Phylotha's "maenadism" for lack of a better term seemed too bizarrely accurate to Euripides to make me wholly comfortable with my theories of drugged wine and narcotics. And there were also Jessamine's earlier descriptions of Phylotha's behaviors to be considered. When I had first read the girl's missive, it had of course passed through my mind that my former fiancée's symptoms sounded similar to descriptions of the Bacchantes from that strangest, most gruesome of plays—her strength, her diet, her aversion to the masculine gaze, her affinity for wild creatures—but I reasoned it must have been a coincidental resemblance. Now, knowing just what preceded her descent…

Yes, there had been discrepancies aplenty in the letters before Cloudsley's, but nothing nearly as fantastical as what he had described—not even the strange circumstances of Vandeleur's murder. And yet—*and yet!* Not everything he related beggared belief. The timing of his report, for example, matched perfectly with what others had confirmed. Dionysios would have had time to converse with Jessamine after Cloudsley's attack (yes, I call it that, though he would not) before hearing Phylotha's screams. And as Phylotha overcame Cloudsley, that was when Dionysios found *me*, ignorant of all he had been through, in the hedge maze. That, at least, I can be certain of.

I was making my way to the center of the maze to sit beside the lovely fountain there. I was exhausted by the events of the evening and the lateness of the hour—it was getting on to three—and longed to take a seat and rest.

When Dionysios padded up behind me, the poor lad was even more disheveled than Jessamine had described in her letter. His clothes were not only torn, but smeared with mud and grass. His beautiful silk cravat was limply hanging about his neck, and his sweet nose had a smudge of something across it. He was panting from his exertions, and looking everywhere, as if searching for something that might as easily be flying through the air as crawling along the ground. He would have run past me without a second glance, I think, but I called out to him. Startled, he whirled around, but relaxed when I hobbled up to him, making more use of my walking stick than I usually must. I put my hand on his shoulder and smiled at him.

"Where are you going? What do you seek so urgently? And what on earth has agitated you so?"

"Thank you for your concern, but I am fine," he replied, with another distracted glance skyward. "I merely seek my master, Mr. Bernard. Have you seen him?"

"No," I said. "Not since I left him and the Count to themselves," I said quickly, seeing Dionysios' obvious desire to leave immediately, yet possessing a keen wish for him to stay with me. "I am headed to the center of this maze. It is quiet there; they might have gone thither to enjoy one another's company just as easily. Why not walk with me a little, and rest yourself? Then we can renew your search."

"All right," he said, clearly reluctant but not wishing to offend. "Thank you, yes, I shall attend you there—but I really must find him soon. It is not for a servant to sit idle when his master may be in want."

"There are servants aplenty to see to everyone's wants, I hope," I said, beginning again to weave my way deeper into the maze. "If not, I have failed as host and as master of this house."

"I meant no disrespect," said Dionysios, as he ambled beside me. "My apologies."

"No need," I said. "You've had a trying time tonight, haven't you?"

He sighed, and clasping his hands behind his back, nodded his head. "In more ways than I anticipated. My visit to Tarrington was out of interest. I traveled quite a long ways to get here, but have been unable to realize my goal."

"I am sorry," I said. "I did not realize you had journeyed so far, and regret you will come away disappointed."

"Very far indeed, and very disappointed."

We had reached the fountain, and with a grunt, I settled myself on the edge of the base. We were alone; the Count and Mr. Bernard were not there, not that I really suspected they would be.

"What a shame," I said, trailing my fingers in the water. "And yet, I envy you. Going somewhere—traveling, I mean, even if in vain, it sounds lovely."

Dionysios laughed softly as he sat beside me, his humor apparently somewhat restored. I fought the urge to move closer to him. He was so very beautiful in the moonlight, on that matter alone were Cloudsley and I in perfect agreement. As at dinner, I felt at peace with him, as if I could be myself with him; that my highest calling in life would be to make him smile.

"Take it from one who knows too well—travel is *awful*," he said. "It's dusty, dirty, uncomfortable, inconvenient, dangerous—to say nothing of how tiresome it is, always eating bad food and sleeping in worse beds, seeing strange faces, nothing certain but the existence of the road ahead and the road behind. Did I say something wrong?"

To hear the one thing I had ever wanted—to see the world—abused so thoroughly! I shook my head, ashamed he had seen my

expression. "Please excuse my weakness," I croaked. "It is only…
well, we always want what we can't have, isn't that human nature?"

"I couldn't say—ah, what I mean is that it's difficult to say.
Some people seem very happy being who they are and doing what
they do. I take it you are not, Mr. Bretwynde?"

"How could I be?" My voice trembled when I spoke. "How
could I be happy, afflicted as I am with my strange disease? It
is a curse, this malady that has made my world smaller than it
ought to be! I have always longed to travel, to explore and see
and learn…but even were I able without laudanum to manage
the cage of pain that is my body, what good would it do me? I
could not see that which I dream of—ancient ruins, rustic castles,
Alpine vistas—by daylight."

"Whatever do you mean?" Dionysios was looking at me keenly,
but I balked at saying more. Despite the above, God knows I try
not to complain to others too often about my myriad symptoms.
But there was sympathy in Dionysios' gaze, and that drew me out.

"My condition, it can be triggered by sunshine. Not only sun,
but wind, and cold. Also not taking enough exercise, or getting
too much, as I have tonight. Or eating too rich a diet."

My companion reached out and put his hand over mine. My
stomach tightened pleasantly at his touch. "I am sorry," he said.
"What are your symptoms?"

"My joints ache. Fever. My hair falls out, and sometimes, my
skin, especially across my cheeks and back, can become red, and
painful."

Dionysios nodded, his eyes two great dark pools. For a moment
I felt dizzy, as though I might be falling into them, and had to
look away.

"It is always difficult, to live feeling you are separate from the
world," he murmured, familiarly squeezing my hand. "I know a
little of what you must endure."

"Do you?"

He hesitated, then nodded. "Mr. Bernard, my employer, is... eccentric. I am not at liberty to discuss exactly *why* I would describe him as such, of course, but some of his habits and tastes are not, let us say, wholly in line with those of other men. I am the only servant he trusts enough with these desires, whims. I am loyal to him, of course, and would not change my situation for the world, but it has often put me in the difficult position of living removed from others. At times, I have been thankful I have no family, for surely they would object to my constantly being at Mr. Bernard's side, but at other times I wonder what I have missed, having no one in the world but him. He raised me from the time I was small. He is all I have."

"So you are well-traveled but hard pressed for company. What an odd combination," I said. "The complete reversal of my own life. I have little familiarity with the world beyond this town— beyond my own home, really, but I never want for society. People are always crowding 'round me, so frequently I wish I could run just to get away from them." I laughed, but not merrily. "I believe my mother is always asking people to Tarrington to try to distract me from myself. She does not believe me when I say I prefer my own society."

A red fox bounded into the enclosed center of the hedge-maze, and, heedless of our presence, leaped forward to land upon some small furry creature of the night. Tossing his head into the air, he swallowed his prey in one gulp, and then looked at us with bright, uncaring eyes. As we watched in companionable silence the creature licked his chops, licked a paw, and strutted out of our view, down one of the lanes of the maze.

"Do you hunt?" asked Dionysios.

"No." I shook my head. "I usually claim the excitement would tax me too severely, but the truth is, I have not the stomach for it. I like foxes and hares and deer; I find watching them more soothing than most other occupations, save reading."

"You have a sweet and tender heart," said Dionysios, in such an adult way it brought a smile to my lips. To hear one so young as he—he whom I could tell was several years my junior—try to speak comfort to me...it made me aware of myself, and I tried to "turn the worm," as it were.

"So do you," I said, withdrawing my hand and patting his knee. "Our earlier conversation about immortality, if you recall...for all you say you would sacrifice those you love to live forever, I cannot believe that is the truth. You are too kind. No, don't try to protest it! You have no chains binding you here, forcing you to sit with a stranger, an *invalid*, in his quiet gardens—but you agreed to come with me, and tarry here yet, though surely you could find greater excitement elsewhere, even at dull Tarrington. That is not something someone who would abandon his friends would do."

"Perhaps you are right." His tone did not match his words. He sniffed, rubbed his nose, and, seeing dirt on his hand, rubbed it again, until it was clean. "Or perhaps I simply do not wish to disillusion you; it is nice to have someone believe such generous sentiments about me."

Though I was enjoying myself thoroughly, I yawned. I could manage my exhaustion no longer, not even for him—and feared, if I further extended myself, I might be ill the next day. Leaning upon my walking stick I gained my feet and offered Dionysios my hand. "Whatever the truth is, you have indulged me, and now let me return the favor. I will walk you back to the house, and leave you to your search. Sadly, I must retire. Dawn is surely not far off."

"Can it be?" Dionysios bit his lip as he allowed me to help him to his feet. "Perhaps it is time for us to get back. I suspect Mr. Bernard will wish us to leave presently."

"Not before tomorrow afternoon, surely!"

"Before dawn, I should think."

My heart began to pound. "You must stay with us longer, I insist! You only just arrived…"

"I have no say in the matter." Dionysios' tone was cooler than before. "I assume my master will wish to depart immediately, our reason for coming being unobtainable."

"What was this reason? You have mentioned it twice, obliquely."

"Have you not intuited the answer? I have often referred to it. We were just speaking of the subject, actually."

I had not, at that point, the benefit of knowing how extensively Dionysios and Jessamine had discussed his obsession with eternal youth—I could only guess, based off our too-brief exchanges. I took a few steps, thinking, and then gasped.

"You really believed you could discover the secret of immortality," I marveled.

Dionysios shrugged. "There are stranger things in this world than a renowned mountebank turning out to be a real magician," he said. "Yes, I had hoped."

I was amazed—amazed and *appalled*. It seemed grossly inappropriate for Mr. Bernard, a man old enough that his salt-and-pepper mustache was well salted indeed, to allow a youth of such tenderness as Dionysios to believe that sort of twaddle. "So it was not your master's notion to come here—it was yours, and he indulged you!"

"Let us say he felt as enthusiastically about the potential as I did," said Dionysios, walking faster now. It became difficult for me to keep up. "But, unless he has discovered something to change his mind in the hours since I saw him last, I know he will require us to depart. The situation with Mr. Welby will force our hand."

"I wish it were not so," I gasped, out of breath.

Dionysios slowed; turned. I looked into his eyes, and again felt lost in his gaze.

"I too regret what must be. But while it may hurt my heart, having found a true compeer here, Julian—Mr. Bretwynde, I mean—I must follow him."

My heart fluttered at his words; hearing him pronounce my Christian name, I felt light-headed and euphoric as I did before I proposed to my once-dear Phylotha. Perhaps, I wondered, he too had felt the strange magnetism between us, and wished he could prolong that sublime sensation. Never had I enjoyed another's company so thoroughly, so quickly, and so explicitly selfishly—even my deep affection for Phylotha was somewhat colored somewhat by duty. Making so bold as to take his hand, as we walked closer and closer to the egress of the maze, I cleared my throat.

"If you speak truly, there could be a place for you here…I know I spoke dismissively of having people about me, but I meant my mother's friends and the doctors who come to shake their heads at me while taking my money. You, I would keep here—if you truly wished to stay, that is. Consider this: Tarrington has an extensive library, with books to satisfy any one of any taste, scientific or literary—and I know my neighbors well enough to borrow anything I do not own. Why, you might find the answers you seek, to your desire for eternal life!" I was grasping at straws, and saw in his expression that this wild idea of mine could never be. "You never know. If you are always traveling, always in motion, you never have time to really sit and learn. Tarrington could give you some much-needed peace."

At the mouth of the maze we paused, my right hand clutching his, and my left, my walking stick. Before us was the house, still ablaze with candle- and torchlight, though oddly quiet; behind us was the maze, shadowed and deceptively empty. Dionysios was clearly unsure whether to retreat into the darkness or emerge into the light. He kept glancing back and forth, failing to meet my eyes as he did so, until I released my walking stick. It fell to the damp grass with a muffled thump as I put my hand on his cheek.

"Dionysios," I said, "think about this. It is possible, what I proposed. We can make it work. And not with you as my servant, no! We could claim you were a distant cousin! A few alterations to your wardrobe, a new wig or two—I would provide it all, of course. You could be a new man. We could even go further than a distant cousin, we could claim you were anything, who would ever know if our history of you is false! Think of it!"

I was enthralled by my own idea, enchanted by it. Only God knows how often I have wished to put aside poor Julian Bretwynde, the invalid—Octavius' son, the disappointment. But looking eagerly at Dionysios, I realized I had said the wrong thing. He pulled away from my touch, eyes narrowed.

"So, you would have me hide myself behind costumes and lies before you even truly know me." I drew back from the bitterness in his voice, and stumbling on a thicker patch of grass, fell on my bottom. I opened my mouth to protest, but no words came. "Yes," he said, not offering me a hand up, but crossing his arms over his chest, "well, you must forgive me if your proposition fails to excite me. I would rather be myself, though I am a servant."

"I did not mean to imply…"

"Of course not. I know. I am simply informing you as to why I cannot accept your…*generous offer.*"

Two figures came up behind Dionysios from the direction of Tarrington. I reached for my cane and tried to haul myself up before they saw me in such an abject pose, but by the time I was on my feet Mr. Bernard was deep in conversation with Dionysios.

"—awake, himself, and very angry, as you predicted," he said. "We should leave immediately, get a few hours distance before dawn. I've been looking for you; where have you been?"

"Lost in the hedge maze," said Dionysios. "Thankfully Mr. Bretwynde was there to show me the way out." He turned to me and bowed formally. "I thank you for your help, but duty calls. Good night, and good bye—as you likely heard, we depart immediately. I must see to the packing."

He strode away, spine straight, chin up. He did not look back.

"I hope you do not view our hasty farewell as rude," said Mr. Bernard, "it is just, ah, Mr. Welby's dismay…"

"I understand perfectly," I said, my voice firm though I felt my heart breaking.

The Count of St. Germain coughed into his fist. "Mr. Bretwynde, let us leave Mr. Bernard to his preparations," he said. "There is an urgent matter which requires your attention."

I shook my head. "My apologies, your lordship, but I am very tired. I must retire."

"I think you will want to delay your plans," he said. "Please—I would not ask were it not of the utmost importance. Will you come?"

The Count was, of course, speaking of Phylotha. When he told me of her condition, though I knew I was pushing myself beyond the limits of my endurance, I went to her, horrified by his description. We both would have been better off had I simply gone to bed. She began screaming and bashing herself against the door when I called her name; overcome with shock, I collapsed, and was unable to rise from bed for three days. By then, my guests, including Dionysios and his master, poor unfortunate Vandeleur, Cloudsley, Jessamine and Phylotha (I heard later they were forced to bind and confine her to a crate), and the Count had all departed. I was alone between doctor's visits, as I had told Dionysios I wished to be, but solitude brought me no peace. I was a man tormented. I could not think of anything beyond the bizarre events of that night, and so, when I had sufficiently recovered, I began this endeavor—though of course, at the time, I did not know I had officially begun it.

No, that came later, much later; in terms of this narrative, it began close to the end.

I had earlier vowed that if Cloudsley's letter did not arrive within three days I would roust myself. I would go to Chidike and, if his story rang true, I would present evidence on his behalf. But that vow was made when I assumed Cloudsley's letter would provide additional facts, rather than additional uncertainty, as to whether Chidike had been wagered that night and thus possessed sufficient motivation to commit a murder.

I still felt it was my duty to hear Chidike's side of things. Knowing the man's qualities, I felt I would be more disposed to believe him than the magistrate—and the magistrate more likely to believe me than him regarding what had occurred. So I told my servants to prepare for a journey to Chittlehampton, making sure the coach was well provisioned and outfitted with the heaviest of shades so I was not forced to endure more sunlight than I was able.

Though the cause of my journey was unfortunate, I was very excited to depart. I had not left Tarrington in close to a year, and only then to visit with Phylotha's family for a fortnight (the trip, at the end of which, I had proposed to her). But ever since my return my mother had begged me not to leave her until my father has arrived back at home, due to a nightmare she experienced whilst I was away, a fantasy wherein Tarrington was a castle, and without a knight to defend her, had fallen to Seljuqs and been sacked. My resolve to attend Chidike displeased her immensely; she pleaded with me not to go for her sake, but I would not be dissuaded. She cited my delicate health, the long hours, the "trifling cause" (as she called it), and even her own prescience—but all in vain. I would go, and did.

I have no words to describe the joy I felt as we went jolting along. To my eyes, even the commonest scenery seemed exotic. The little traveling-shelters in various states of repair, fences I had not seen for months, stands of beech-trees, lakes clogged with reeds and twittering birds, houses I had never visited…when I spied a magnificent hart I gasped aloud, and had Kirwin stop the coach, but the fine fellow leaped away as soon as he noticed us.

But after a few hours, as we drew nearer to Hatherleigh, the landscape lost some of its charm. I knew somewhere nearby Vandeleur had been overpowered, murdered, and partially consumed. When we stopped for a quick picnic tea in the shade of a spreading oak, I asked Kirwin if he knew exactly where the crime had been committed.

"Only a few miles from here, Mr. Bretwynde," he replied. "My cousin Kilcoursie shewed me the spot when last I came this way. We'll pass by there before too long."

"Is that so?" I chewed thoughtfully on a thick piece of cold cured tongue and mustard. Thinking on what became of my poor cousin, I said, "How dreadful."

"Sorry, Mr. Bretwynde," said Kirwin. "The only other way 'round would take us days out of our way."

"No no, you mistake me," I said quickly. "I meant how dreadful what befell Mr. Welby. I should like to see the place, actually."

"I'll stop when we get there," he promised.

Not long after resuming our travels I felt the carriage slow, and Kirwin indicated we had reached the fatal glade. I donned my broadest-brimmed tricorne and stepped onto the roadside. It was wholly unremarkable; the place should have held no interest for me whatsoever save for my knowledge of what had happened there.

I rambled to and fro amongst the pines, poking at the earth with my stick wherever it seemed unnaturally disturbed. I saw little beyond what Mrs. Welby had described. There was a rough hut, a stout tree with a low branch where it would likely have been convenient to hang poor Vandeleur to drain, a firepit where his arms were likely cooked…but whoever had found his remains had cleaned up thoroughly. Nothing of the crime could be detected—at least, so I thought, until the sun came out from behind a cloud and I spied something that glinted at me in the underbrush.

"Mr. Bretwynde," called Kirwin. "Don't linger too long, we want to be at The George before dark."

"Give me a moment," I said, and pushed my way through the brambles and low branches to see if I could uncover whatever it was that gleamed so very brightly.

It was a long strand of polished copper links and red coral beads, half-covered by fallen leaves. It was not a valuable piece of jewelry—not objectively speaking. But as I had seen it before, and knew its worth to its owner, I assumed it had been abandoned in haste, and picked it up in the hopes of returning it. The ornaments slipped from the horsehair on which they were strung, so kneeling, I scooped up all the bangles I could find and secreted them in the pocket of my coat.

The next day I arrived in Chittlehampton, and after a restful night's sleep, I rose and breakfasted early, with the intention of immediately visiting the jail where Chidike languished.

When I arrived, I was disgusted. Chidike looked as poorly as a beggar—gaunt, filthy, and downcast. When I called his name, he barely roused himself.

"My dear fellow!" I exclaimed. "I say, jailer! Bring me a basin and a good breakfast immediately, and a change of clothes for this man. You should be ashamed of yourself! I have never seen—never *heard* of—such abuse and neglect."

I may be a weakling, but I can summon a sufficiently lordly

imperiousness when I must. My tone sent scurrying the black-guard who, when I entered the jail, was throwing playing cards into his hat instead of attending his charges. Soon enough he returned with hot water, soap, and a cloth, and after letting me in to Chidike's miserable cell, went off again in search of a decent repast.

"Here, let me help you," I said, beginning to sponge off his face and neck. Too quickly the water became fouled, but by the end of my ministrations, Chidike was a sight cleaner and much more coherent. After changing his clothes and forcing down the better part of a flagon of beer, a bowl of oatmeal, and some bacon, he was very nearly recovered, though still frail.

"I had no idea of the direness of your circumstances," I swore. "I was ill, and heard only that you were to be tried—which I attempted to forestall with promises of coming myself to testify on your behalf."

"You should have let them hang me," said Chidike.

"Steady," I said. "I'm here now, and better late than never, eh? I came to hear your side of all of this, as I know you are not the sort of man to butcher a fellow creature. After I know the details I shall speak to the magistrate and make a case for your immediate release."

"And you think that will work?"

"Of course! I mean, we both know you were there, but I'm sure you weren't the one to commit those dastardly acts de-scribed to me by your former mistress."

Chidike canted his head to the right. "We both know I was there? How is that?"

I reached into my coat pocket and withdrew his bracelet. In pieces though it was, he gasped at the sight of it, and let me pour the contents of my palm into his.

"I never thought to see my mother's prayer beads again," he

murmured. "Thank you, Mr. Bretwynde. Wherever did you find them?"

"In the wood behind the hut."

He sighed. "Well, I suppose I must now tell you all, whatever may happen as a result. You are already hurting my case, however—I have been claiming I was not there at all."

This did not bode well, no it did not. "Why ever would you say such a thing?"

"Because the lie was more believable than the truth." He looked at me, and to my delight I saw a hint of his former archness. "It is a long story, Mr. Bretwynde. Do you think you could prevail upon that most hated of jailers for another flagon of something to ease my throat? Otherwise I fear I shall be hoarse by the end of the telling."

At that point I was desiring some sort of nuncheon, so I demanded a cold collation be brought to us. When it arrived, we made quick work of the simple but nourishing fare, and Chidike settled in to tell me all, as he puffed on one of my cigars.

"That's better," he said. "I must enjoy every one of life's pleasures while I can. Ah, but before I begin, I must beg you to hear me out. I am certain you will find the story improbable, if not impossible."

"Perhaps before that fateful night," I said. "In the wake of it, I have learned I know less about the world than I realized. Please tell me all."

I should make a note here that what follows is not what Chidike told me in that dreary cell; rather, it is a statement he wrote with his own hand at my request, later on. They differ but little, so instead of recording the same events twice, I choose instead to place his account here:

I know too well what I compose here will not be believed—is not believed—not even by the one who asked me to write it down. The tale is too extraordinary. But I swear it is completely true. Were I born an Englishman, I think my peers would seek to label me mad, claiming what I claim—but I am not an Englishman. No, instead my allegations will be attributed to my race, for I know too well the tendency of your sort to ascribe to mine a predisposition to fanciful beliefs and a primitive, atavistic mindset.

It is said by my accusers that I killed Mr. Welby, cut off his arms, roasted them, consumed them, and then ran away from the scene of the crime in order to hide my guilt. It is said I committed these vile acts in anger, after Mr. Welby wagered and lost me at cards. And yet, what my accusers say is not accurate, save that I did indeed run from the place he was murdered. Yes, I was there, and saw what occurred. I admit that at first, I told a falsehood about the events of that morning—I claimed I ran away earlier than I did, and had no knowledge of what befell him. But it will presently become clear why I lied, when I reveal what truly happened.

The theory presented by my accusers falters at its inception. It was Nineveh, not myself, which was wagered away that night. Mr. Bernard—he who won Nineveh—expressly turned down my person as a prize equivalent to his own manservant Dionysios, when initially I was offered. Though chattel, I am separate from Mr. Welby's Jamaica holdings. I belong to him, not to the plantation. Thus I remained in Mr. Welby's service upon Mr. Bernard receiving the deed of ownership.

While the Count of St. Germain's stratagem may have worked to distract Mr. Welby from his rancor, I wonder if it would not have been better to have the two gentlemen settle the matter with a simple duel.

Upon seeing the direction the night was headed I retired early to read and sleep rather than attend the revels. There were enough servants about to serve everyone, including Mr. Welby, who seemed disinclined to be waited upon anyways. My direct knowledge begins when, shortly after three in the morning, I was shaken awake by Mr. Welby. He had obviously not been to bed at all. His clothing was in a state, his wig missing, his hair uncombed, and his eyes were bloodshot and shining with a manic light I did not like at all.

"Up with you, Chidike!" he cried, startling me. "Dress yourself! We ride! We ride for glory, and for justice!"

I rubbed at my eyes; I had been very deeply asleep, and his shouting confounded me. "Whatever do you mean, sir?"

"Get yourself up and into traveling clothes, and find my hunting-coat." He began to pace the room like some caged beast. "He has fled, but I mean to catch him."

"To whom do you refer, sir?" I went to our closet to find Mr. Welby a suitable coat, knowing we had not brought our hunting-clothes with us.

"That rogue Bernard, of course," he spat. "He left with the note I signed, and I shan't let him get away with it. Amounts to theft, really—he must know I could never allow him to *really* keep Nineveh."

I said nothing. It had been a foolish wager to make, and if Mr. Bernard meant to keep his spoils, well, many might think him cruel, but fewer still would hand back a fortune such as that, won fairly.

I helped Mr. Welby dress warmly in sturdy clothing, including buckling on our customized bandolier that held our two flintlock dueling pistols—though I will note here that I advised against him wearing them. I thought it unwise, while pursuing someone with whom one wished to conduct a peaceful negotiation, to appear heavily armed. But Mr. Welby did not heed my advice; indeed, he demanded I cease offering further opinions, so I dressed myself in silence.

"We will overtake them easily, I think," said Mr. Welby, as a bleary-eyed groom readied two horses. It was quarter till four in the morning; dawn was not yet imminent, so the night air was chilly, and dense with swirling mist. "They only have a half-hour's start on us, and are in a coach. If we ride fast it should be no trouble to catch them. Once we have the deed we can ride back—why, I wager we'll return in time for breakfast!"

I did not point out that Mr. Welby's wagers had not been proven particularly sound of late. No, I merely helped him onto his horse, and before I could even get into the saddle he was off like a shot. I followed as well as I was able, but Mr. Welby was riding like the devil himself was after him. It was all I could do to keep him in my sights when the road was straight, for my horse was not as fine, and sleepy, and as disinclined to heed my instructions to hurry as I was to give them.

When the east was just beginning to show signs of brightening Mr. Bernard's carriage at last came into sight. Mr. Welby let go a triumphal whoop and dug his spurs into the lathered flanks of his horse. The poor creature screamed, reared, and took off again. For my part, I kept my distance. Our ride had given me even more time to muse on how bad this plan of Mr. Welby's truly was. And yet, as quickly became evident, even my imagination was mild in comparison to what really occurred.

"Ho there!" cried Mr. Welby, cantering up alongside the coach. From the slightness of the figure on the riding board, I assumed it was the lad Dionysios holding the reins. "Slow down! It's me, Vandeleur Welby."

The driver did indeed slow the coach. As I trotted up I saw the shade rise, and Mr. Bernard's profile emerge from the carriage window.

"Good morning, Mr. Welby. You followed me? How extraordinary!" Mr. Bernard sounded amused. "What on earth could you want?"

"To talk," said Mr. Welby. "Come now, let us discuss some business. I know it's unusual, but what else could I do? You stole away from Tarrington like a thief in the night."

"Stole? Thief?" Mr. Bernard stuck his entire head out the window. "Denys! Find a likely place and let us pull over."

Dionysios looked back, his thin black brows drawn together. "It is very close to dawn, Mr. Bernard."

"I am aware. Don't worry; this won't take long."

Mr. Welby seemed to take comfort in this. "Very good," he said. "I knew you'd be reasonable."

"Did you? How nice." Mr. Bernard pulled his head back inside his coach, and yanked down the shade.

Eventually we stopped beside a small travelers' hut. Dionysios leaped off the riding board, tethered the horses, and let Mr. Bernard out as I saw to our steeds. Mr. Welby's in particular was in a bad state, foaming, champing, and in quite a temper. I told Mr. Welby I would lead them to the stream I heard burbling somewhere deeper in the chill, foggy wood, but he barely heard me, for he was distracted, eager to engage in conversation with Mr. Bernard.

Both horses were very thirsty, but I did not let them drink too much; the water was quite cold. My horse, who was neither exhausted nor offended by rough treatment, obeyed me when I clicked at him and pulled away his nose. Mr. Bernard's steed, however, was cross, and snapped at me. Throwing my horse's reins around a branch, I spoke quietly and calmly to Mr. Bernard's, but the beast was not to be reasoned with.

I was at the end of my patience dealing with the creature when I heard Mr. Welby yelp—and then heard a surprised, dampened end to his cry, as if someone had muffled him. It made my hair stand up on end. The sound was odd enough to spook his horse—it neighed, and, leaping the stream, took off into the murky forest, and was soon gone from my sight. I, on the other hand, elected not to rush any-where, much less back to the hut; if the two gentlemen had ganged up on the one, injuring Mr. Welby, I assumed my assistance would be most appreciated by getting Mr. Welby back to Tarrington than getting into a brawl. Thus, I crept softly back to the roadside, taking care to make as little noise as possible.

Someone had enkindled a fire, and it winked merrily at me through the trees. Its popping and cracking aided me as well, for it hid the odd snap of a twig under my foot. I was afraid of what violence I might discover, so I kept my distance, and elected to climb a tree to obtain the best possible view. Yet after shimmying up a convenient alder, I regretted my choice, for upon beholding what was happening I nearly let go in alarm, and skinned my shin and palms in my haste to grab hold of the trunk once again. It is then that I must have lost my mother's beads.

They were all three there. Dionysios was squatting beside a fire, which he was stirring with a stick. I was shocked to see my master lying on the ground, on his back, with Mr. Bernard kneeling over him. At first, I could not ascertain what he could be doing; soon enough Mr. Bernard stood, and when he looked up I tell you the gentleman's face was covered in blood. He had been drinking from Mr. Welby's sliced-open throat. His lips were coated with gore from his unholy feast, and when he spoke, I saw his teeth were black and fouled.

"He's nearly drained," said Mr. Bernard, wiping his mouth with the back of his gloved hand. "How's the fire?"

"Coals won't be ready before sunup," said Dionysios.

"Hmm. Well, I must retire presently."

"I know. I suppose soup would—" Dionysios looked up, brow furrowed. "What happened to his man? His slave, I mean? Didn't he go off to water their horses?"

Mr. Bernard shrugged, then went back to slurping from Mr. Welby's neck.

"I don't like this," said Dionysios. "He should have come back by now. I'm going to go look for him."

Mr. Bernard did not look up; he waved Dionysios away with his red-soaked hand.

"Be careful. Get inside before daybreak even if I'm not—"

"I know what I'm about," Mr. Bernard gurgled testily through a mouthful of blood.

"Fine." Dionysios withdrew a large folding knife from his waistcoat pocket. He flicked it open, and it gleamed in the firelight as he cast about in all directions, peering through the mist. Thankfully I was up above where he was looking, but I kept as still as I could, even holding my breath when he passed beneath me. That, I think, was the most terrifying moment of all, for had he spied me—I shall not speculate.

After Dionysios had disappeared into the wood I returned my attention to the gruesome Mr. Bernard. He was still pulling and sucking at Mr. Welby's throat, making awful little sounds, smacking his lips and grunting like a hog at a trough. I thought he was emitting little cries, as well, but I realized soon enough that Mr. Welby was not yet dead; he, not Mr. Bernard, was whimpering. I had to look away.

"Was it worth it?" Mr. Bernard asked the now pale, lifeless body. "I can't imagine your plantation was worth dying for, but then again, that's not the sort of calculation I have to make."

"Calculation?" Dionysios had returned to the clearing.

"Deciding if something is worth dying for." Mr. Bernard seemed pleased with himself.

"I couldn't find Mr. Welby's slave," said Dionysios. "No sign of him anywhere. There was a horse tied to a tree, though."

"Only the one?"

Dionysios nodded. "I crossed the stream; there were hoofprints on the other side that led into the forest. Perhaps he took the opportunity to run off. I just wish I knew what he saw before he fled."

"Likely nothing at all. Goodness knows I'd take the first opportunity to run were I in his position." Dionysios did not look pleased by this statement, but he said nothing. "It's time I was in bed. Do you need any help?"

"It would be lovely if you would get off his arms for me."

"Ah. Of course."

As if I had not seen enough uncannyness, Mr. Bernard, seemingly without effort, tore Mr. Welby's arms off at the shoulder, like a man might disengage the wing of a roast chicken. He then tipped his hat to his manservant and climbed inside his carriage. I did not see him again.

Dionysios idled by the fire, poking it, stirring the coals, intermittently checking the road to ensure no one was coming upon him. I prayed he would hurry, for I was freezing and my legs were cramping, but he took his time, even making a rudimentary spit with some forked branches so he could roast the arms together, turning them occasionally as he stamped his feet and slapped his arms upon his breast to keep warm.

Eventually the boy, if boy he was, removed his terrible repast from the fire. After wrapping up one arm in Mr. Welby's shirt, he made a meal of the other. He stripped the meat from the bones with his knife and then chewed the bones clean, even going so far as to crack them and suck out the marrow. After he had finished he tossed the remains into the fire, wiped his hands clean on Mr. Welby's trouser-legs, and kicked dirt over the coals, pissing on them to make sure they were thoroughly out. The steam was noisome but I endured it without coughing, for I knew to give myself away now was to suffer the same fate. Or worse...

There is not much to tell after that. Dionysios tossed Mr. Welby's other arm upon the riding board, and after untying the reins from where they held the horses, he clambered up, and drove away into the dawn.

I waited a long time after that to climb down, sore as I have ever been, and crept to my horse. Yes, I fled, and hid myself until I was noticed at Chittlehampton market and arrested for Mr. Welby's murder and desecration.

I did not report the murder as I did not think it would do anything but hasten my arrest, given the

outlandish nature of the crime—and indeed, my
suspicions have been borne out. The one person
to whom I have confessed the whole of the matter,
though an acquaintance of some years, expressed not
a little skepticism over the details. Not that I blame
him. I likely would have reacted the same had he
been the one telling me the tale.

That is all. Everything. As I said, I know this report
will not be believed, but it is true. I am not mad, nor
am I some primitive-minded creature. Mr. Welby
more than once had cause to call me cold, a skeptic.
But it is far easier to hang me than to seek that which
dwells not in darkness, but among us, passing as one
of us, but apart from us. That would take far more
courage than I know my accusers possess.

But perhaps I am not one to speak of courage, I
who hid whilst all this carnage and waste happened
before my eyes. I do not know, and worse, I do not
know if I care. Likely the liberty to ponder such
imponderables will be taken from me.

***

I wish I could deny Chidike's assertion that I found his story
impossible, but at first, as I listened to him speak, I was more
than skeptical. I could not make myself believe that Mr. Bernard
would kill my cousin Vandeleur by sucking out his life's blood
through his throat, and Dionysios eat of his flesh! It all seemed
beyond the probable, to say the very least.

But perhaps the mad contents of Cloudsley's missive had soft-
ened me up, for I found myself questioning my initial impulse to
dismiss Chidike entirely. I forced myself to consider more than

his words—the sincerity of his delivery mattered, after all, as did the reliability of the source. I have never known Chidike to lie, and he did not speak as one lying. No, he related all of this in something like a daze, as if it had happened a very long time ago, yet he appeared certain of every detail.

"Well, Mr. Bretwynde?" he asked.

I jumped a little. I had been staring at my feet as I contemplated his various accusations.

"Chidike—"

"I know." He was perfectly calm, unnaturally so. He took a final drag on his cigar and ground it out under his heel. "You cannot credit my story. Honestly, were our fortunes reversed—"

"It's not that. It's just...not three hours before you say you saw Dionysios gnaw a man's arm down to the marrow he was sitting quietly with me in my own gardens, his hand on mine, speaking words of comfort." I bit my lip, remembering the warmth of his touch—but also the cold light in his eyes when he looked down at me as I knelt in the grass.

It occurred to me that I was weighing the sensations I experienced in the company of a youth whom I had known for but a few short hours against the word of a man whose society I had enjoyed for the better part of a decade, and whose honor I had seen tested and never judged wanting. Chidike had always been a reliable fellow, whereas I knew nothing at all about Dionysios, save for his wish to live forever. But I knew one thing for certain—and I knew what I had to do.

Chidike was looking out the narrow window that let in only a single beam of the afternoon sunlight. I followed his line of sight, watching the motes drift hither and yon for a time, and then cleared my throat.

"My dear fellow, I have done you an injustice." He looked over at me. "Chidike, whether I believe every part of your story is irrelevant, for I do not believe you capable of committing the crime of which you are accused. I will go directly to the magistrate to make an appeal on your behalf, and do everything in my power to see you freed. Your word is enough for me. I would not be a gentleman if I did not defend you in your hour of need."

"Mr. Bretwynde." Just those words conveyed so much. Chidike was looking at me with the queerest expression I had ever seen on his face. He looked more incredulous than I must have during his description of watching Mr. Bernard's unlikely method of murdering my cousin, which is saying something—but he also seemed rather touched. I cannot say he displayed any appearance of having confidence in me, but then again, his situation was such that perhaps he sensed the word of a gentleman might not be enough to clear his name.

"Tomorrow I shall call on Judge Surrow first thing and demand to be heard. I shall tell him…well, I shan't tell him *all* you told me, lest he doubt my sanity. But I shall tell him that not only do I know you could not possibly have committed this murder, but that you had no motivation to do so. I was there when the wagering was done, and know for a fact that you were not at stake. Furthermore, I shall tell him that I trust enough in your character to offer you a place in my household upon your release, for it seems unlikely that whatever the outcome Mrs. Welby will likely not wish you back in her service. That, I think, should show him how much faith I have in your innocence."

"We shall see if it is enough," said Chidike wryly, before adding, "I certainly hope so. Thank you very much."

As I write this, I have no notion if my efforts were successful. Judge Surrow heard me out, but even though he said I presented a decent case, he still sent Chidike on to the Crown Court. Whether he will be hanged or released into my care, I do not know, but I fear the worst. Here is what happened:

Salcome Surrow was still breakfasting when I called upon him the next morning, and drunk—not completely, but certainly impressively, considering the hour. When I heard he was still at his table, and smelled the beer and bacon, I had hopes that perhaps such a large breakfast would make him amiable, like how tigers and lions said to be more docile after a heavy meal. I was not disappointed.

"Oh, it's you," was his greeting, when I was shown in to his dining room. "You've caused me quite a lot of trouble and not a little expense. I am eager to be done with the matter. The people don't like it when things take this long. They consider it a waste of public funds."

"When I saw Chidike he was half-starved. Surely you could not have been wasting too much money on him."

"Yes, well, food isn't the only expense with a prisoner, is it? None of the other criminals will share a cell with him, so we've had to rent—"

"I'm sorry, your worship, but I didn't come all this way to discuss Chidike's room and board." Seeing Judge Surrow's expression sour I moderated my tone. "Rather, I came to discuss his guilt or innocence."

"Yes, of course," he said, pulling the tablecloth from his collars and pushing his chair back. "All right, all right. Come with me, and I'll hear what you have to say."

I spoke for perhaps half an hour, relating in as much detail as I could my confidence in Chidike's character, my certainty that he lacked the motivation to commit murder and worse, and everything else. To his credit, Judge Surrow listened attentively, nodding at various points in my narrative. When I finished he sighed, belched, excused himself, and shook his head.

"Well, Mr. Bretwynde, I cannot disregard your vouching for Chidike—not only because of what you say, but who you are.

The problem is…"

"Yes?"

"Well, it is a matter of jurisdiction. While this has obviously been under my purview until now, the severity of the crime—and the lack of additional suspects—means I feel I cannot rule on the matter. I can make a recommendation to the Crown Court, of course, but as to influencing their decision…"

"But you could dismiss the charges entirely," I protested. "There *are* alternative suspects; as I said, I can corroborate Chidike's claim that he and Mr. Welby left in pursuit of Mr. Bernard and his servant—and as they have disappeared, perhaps under the names Silvanus Blofeld and Teyssandier Vicars, with known intent to voyage to Jamaica, the sooner that matter is pursued, the sooner the true culprits may be brought to justice."

"I cannot assume their guilt any more than I can assume your friend Chidike's innocence," said the magistrate. "Nor can I dismiss Mrs. Welby's assertions in light of your statement, for both amount essentially to hearsay. I'm sorry, but I have not the authority to decide his fate." He sighed. "Mr. Bretwynde, you are to be commended for the time and effort you have spent pursuing this matter. I cannot say I would have done the same for a cousin's slave. I do wonder, however, how much further are you willing to go for the poor fellow?"

"As far as is necessary—I will do all I can to prevent the execution of an innocent man."

"Then I have a recommendation for you," replied Judge Surrow. "You told me of your difficulties traveling, so I assume going further afield for an indefinite period of time will be beyond your abilities. Well, the next best thing would be for you to make a written statement and submit it to me. I shall ensure it is sent along with everything else."

I agreed to this and took my leave of the man, feeling somewhat defeated, but not entirely unhopeful. Surrow seemed a reasonable fellow. But I found, once I had returned to my room at the Golden Lion and sat down with pen and paper before me, I knew not how to begin. At the end of two hours I had collected so many false starts I could have saved on a month's kindling at Tarrington with the pile of crumpled efforts I had tossed upon the floor. Every attempt seemed incomplete, hollow; a meager piece of unbleached muslin when held beside the rich tapestry of my memories.

Deciding to consult with Chidike on this matter, I sallied forth once again to the jail with a few of my aborted attempts in hand. I asked him to look over them for me and see if he could pinpoint where I was going wrong.

"I'm confused," he said, after perusing the pages, "why you seem to be compiling an account of the entire night, when the magistrate is only interested in my case in particular? I do not mean to be rude, but all this about your mother observing the Count of St. Germain's magic in London and whatnot...how does it bear upon the matter at hand?"

"Oh...well, you know, I had tried to begin with the wager, but without knowing the character of Dionysios, and Mr. Bernard, and the Count of St. Germain, and Vandeleur too, it seemed wanting on detail."

Perhaps sensing my discomfort, Chidike set aside the pages and looked me in the eye. "You are not compiling an account to supplement your own memory of the night," he said gently, "you are writing a statement for a court of law. They will want details...but not all of this. Mr. Bretwynde, I appreciate your obvious wish to do the most you can for me, but if I may be so bold, exhausting a judge with extraneous details will likely hurt my case more than help it."

"I see." His critique stung, but I saw the truth of it. "You are correct on both counts, I think. I *am* worried the details of that night will fade, but it is likely true all of this will do nothing to help you." I did not add that I feared I had already forgotten much, as was typical for me, due to my necessary reliance on laudanum. "Well, I shall try again, and narrow my focus."

"Why not do both?" Chidike handed back my papers. "If you are still willing, complete your statement and save all of this for your own edification. Personally, I cannot see why you would wish to remember that night at all, but from what you have told me of your correspondence with others in attendance, it has clearly been a personal quest of yours for some time. Why not acknowledge your desire and turn all of this into something like a diary? It might prove cathartic for you, at the very least."

"By Jove!" I cried. "Chidike, you really are the smartest fellow I know." I sobered quickly, however. The notion that a man of his discernment and wit being put to death for no reason…I resolved then I would start over, and do my absolute best for him. "You're right, and that is exactly what I shall do. Thank you for your counsel."

"It is my pleasure." He stood; I took his hint, and followed suit. "My apologies, but if you will excuse me, the hour is late…"

"Of course. I shall return when I have delivered my statement to Judge Surrow. But…" I hesitated.

"Yes?"

"If I am to make a full account of that night, I would be remiss in not including your experience." I blushed, I know not why. "Would you be so good to write it down for me, if I brought you pen and paper?"

"Of course," said Chidike. "It is the least I can do to thank you. And, really, it will be a comfort to me to know there is a full and accurate account of what I beheld *somewhere*."

I blushed again. I had not told Chidike that I believed it unwise to include any of the more sordid details of his story in my letter to Judge Surrow, but he must have intuited my intent. I felt I was doing so for his own good, but I think he took it as a sign I did not believe him. Which, to be fair, I did not—or rather, I did not know what to believe.

"Do not trouble yourself, Mr. Bretwynde," he said, as if sensing my discomfort. "I myself said that no one would believe me—did I not tell you that is the exact reason I felt it prudent to lie at first, about being at the scene of the crime at all? I appreciate your help, but you must understand—if I seem bitter it is because, quite frankly, I *am*. I have no alibi save for an unbelievable story, no defense except the sworn statement of one man who was not there. Would you change places with me?"

"Truthfully, not for the world," I said. "I am sorry about all of this, my friend."

The next day I carefully wrote the most convincing statement I could, and for good measure hand-delivered two copies to Judge Surrow. Somewhat less intoxicated than during our first meeting, he thanked me, and vowed he would let me know whatever he heard from the Crown Court. It still saddened me that he had decided to pass the case along, but I took comfort knowing I had done my best.

Still, after collecting Chidike's account and saying farewell, it was not with a particularly light heart that I began my journey back to Tarrington. I had failed to acquit Chidike, which had been my hope—and not only that, but upon speaking with him, I found I had more questions rather than fewer. At least I held out hope that beginning—and completing—this archive would straighten it all out in my mind. At the very least, working on it kept me from the very darkest of my thoughts; it has been an excellent distraction from my pain.

Within a week I had penned much of what is written here,

but felt the record was incomplete for two reasons. First, I had no copies of my own letters, only approximations of what I had written. Thus, I sent requests to all my correspondents, politely requesting the return of what I had sent them. Obviously, only some complied; for those who did not I had to create the best facsimiles as I could manage in lieu of the documents themselves.

The second reason I found my account wanting was that I realized there was a great and inexcusable hole in it. This occurred to me only whilst reading over Chidike's report. My feelings were still intensely conflicted as regarded his accusations toward Dionysios—but realized I felt nearly nothing at all regarding what he had to say about Mr. Bernard. Well, that is not entirely true. I was obviously horrified by the allegation that the man may have killed my cousin in cold blood and done unspeakable things to his person; I mean simply that I had no personal feelings about it being *Mr. Bernard* who committed these acts. I had had no intimate interactions with the man, so—unlike with Dionysios—I had no ability to compare Chidike's account with my own. It was a weakness in my researches, and it disturbed me to have my attempt at thoroughness end in such failure.

How, then, to rectify this situation? I tried to recall who amongst my guests kept Mr. Bernard company during the course of his short stay. Cloudsley sat at the cards-table with him, certainly, but as my former friend refused to respond even to my request for my letter to be returned, I doubted I could get him to give me his read on Mr. Bernard specifically. Vandeleur, of course, had perished, and his wife had met only "Teyssandier Vicars," never his master. My other correspondents, Jessamine and Lady Nerissa, had scarcely, or utterly failed to notice the man. Which left only one person in all my acquaintance whom I could ask.

Whether I could actually locate the Count of St. Germain was doubtful; whether I could induce him to respond, even more so.

I knew he had intended to go from Devon to Radstock, where he was to spend some time entertaining the Walcome-Starlings, a prominent family in that area. My fear was that so much time having passed between his departure from Tarrington and my wishing to contact him that he would have already taken his leave for parts unknown. But, nothing ventured, so the saying goes. I composed this missive (copying the contents into this book before sending it):

> The Count of St. Germain
> Falchion Abbey
> Radstock
> Somerset

> Your Lordship,
> I sincerely hope this letter reaches you. It has long disturbed me that due to my illness I was unable to properly thank you for your visit and see you off from Tarrington. It was never my wish that you should come away from my house feeling that the hospitality and courtesy due to you were in any way lacking. I hope one day you are able to return to Devon, and I can make up to you whatever discourtesies you may feel have been done to you.
> It seems impolite to pair an apology with a request, but circumstances being what they are, I must risk your displeasure and hope for your mercy. I am unsure if you have heard about the various unpleasant incidents that have occurred in the wake of your visit, but even after Miss Mallory's episode and my collapse, there were yet further tragedies. My cousin Mr. Welby left Tarrington, pursuing Mr. Bernard on

horseback, and was murdered early that morning for his trouble. My cousin's widow has attempted to blame Mr. Welby's manservant Chidike, but I disbelieve he is the culprit.

It has been suggested that it was actually Mr. Bernard who killed Mr. Welby, a theory of the crime that makes more sense than an attack by Chidike, given their high-stakes wagering the night before—though of course I am not accusing Mr. Bernard, merely attempting to thoroughly contextualize my questions for you. If you would be kind enough to humor me, your Lordship, I would know your opinion of Mr. Bernard.

I assure you, I will keep your words a secret; I would not dream of presenting anything you told me in confidence in a court of law. Indeed, my involvement with the affair is largely over. I have already supplied a written deposition on Chidike's behalf, and do not believe I will be called upon to testify due to my frailty. Furthermore, I suspect Mr. Bernard has already departed for Jamaica, and is thus beyond anyone's reach.

No, I wish to know your opinion of him for reasons of my own. I did not speak much with the man during his short stay at Tarrington; I had more of a chance to become acquainted with his servant. But strange allegations have been made against Mr. Bernard—allegations I do not like to repeat, for their ghastly, unsettling, and unprovable nature—and without knowing more of the man, I find I do not know what to think. So much queerness occurred that night, under my own roof and on my grounds that I feel the need to try to make sense of it all for my own peace of mind.

I am asking you, for I know you attended Mr. Bernard—or rather, he attended *you*—during those early morning hours. As far as I have been able to ascertain, no one else associated with the man so intimately, making you the only person I can ask. And frankly, your Lordship, I would wish to consult you on this matter and others even were that not the case.

Speaking with friends who beheld the results of your entertainment in the garden that night, and learning more of the nature of Miss Mallory's ongoing affliction, I am curious to know exactly what transpired. Let me be frank, your Lordship: while I longed to believe my mother's accounts of the various miracles you performed in London this past season, please do not take offense to know I was skeptical, and interested to see your performances so I might judge for myself. But, like so much that occurred that night, I find that now all is said and done I am more confused, rather than less.

I cannot imagine you are in the habit of divulging your secrets, but given the aftermath of that evening I implore you to enlighten me—if not for my sake, then Miss Phylotha Mallory's. She has not recovered, and if there is something you know that could help her, I beg you to reveal it.

Again, my apologies for asking more of you than I already have. I pray for your forbearance, and for a reply.

Your humble servant,

Julian Bretwynde

Having just this morning put this missive into my valet's care, I must now abandon this pursuit until such a time as I hear from the Count of St. Germain. Without a letter from him I fear this endeavor will always feel incomplete, though I know I have done the best job possible. Hopefully he will take pity on me, and allow me to put the matter completely to rest. Until then I must find a way to occupy myself, a way to put these troubles behind me for a time—or forever, if he should not favor me with a response. Only time will tell whether this has all been in vain.

***

St. Germain's answer has come. I never hoped to receive such a speedy reply from him; indeed, I tried not to hope for one at all, though of course I longed to hear whatever he would tell me. And yet, now that I have read what he has to say, I wish I had never conceived the idea to write to him at all.

The Count was indeed still residing with the Walcome-Starlings when my letter arrived, facilitating our communication. Where he has gone from there, I know not—I believe he redacted that information on purpose, not wishing this conversation to continue. He should not have worried. Even if he had been bound for my neighbor's I would not have sought him out; were he staying adjacent to me in an inn I should not consider knocking on his door. No, I am finished with him, and with this affair. I have realized too late that my quest has brought only heartache, and obtaining all this information, rather than illuminating anything, has instead served to confound and disturb me all the more.

I doubt I shall ever wish to open this folio in future, but I know it will nag at me were I to leave out his response. No, I must paste it in, and not burn it, as was my first impulse:

My dearest Mr. Bretwynde,

Child, let me first and foremost beg you not to trouble yourself further on account of what you perceive as a lack of hospitality. I understand too well the plagues and illnesses of mankind, and the toll they take on those who suffer from them. I was never offended by your inability to personally attend and accompany me during the final days of my stay at Tarrington. While the delightful society of your mother and the attentiveness of your servants did not replace your convivial presence, I was never left wanting for comfort or company.

Let me also immediately offer my condolences for the loss of your cousin, Mr. Welby. Though I knew him for only a brief period, he seemed a most interesting individual, and his participation in the evening's entertainments was perhaps the finest display of man's ability to channel the sublime that I have ever had the privilege to witness. He was supremely adaptable, physically and mentally, to the spirit-realm's influence, producing, you must concede, some most astonishing results.

I am truly saddened to hear of his untimely death, for he saved my life—and I, I am sad to say, played a part in ending his—which is why your desire for my counsel troubles me. I wonder if anything I might say would heal this wound you carry. But, having begun, I may as well finish, I suppose...

Yes, I spent more time with Mr. Bernard than anyone else. He intrigued me with his dramatic entrance during our discussion of immortality, and his subsequent behavior did little to diminish my fascination. For example, the young man to whom you were speaking at the time, his page Dionysios—he seemed positively desperate to serve Mr. Bernard. That sort of devotion in one's servants is only obtained via committing great acts of violence upon them or obtaining their adamant love. Sometimes both, I suppose. Regardless, your fondness for the lad makes me hope it was the latter, but I have my concerns. The man did not exactly give me cause to believe in his fundamental goodness; no, he was positively Luciferian, as magnificent, as facile a speech-maker—and as inspiring of feelings, including misguided devotion.

I have said the man piqued my interest, but perhaps I ought to say that we aroused one another's curiosity. Surely you noticed, after joining the ladies but before I began my concert, that Mr. Bernard sought my particular company? He did this by playing on a known love of mine: gemstones. As I sat with the younger Miss Mallory, who if I recall correctly was very concerned my concert might go on too long, he presented me with an amethyst ring.

"Your lordship," he said, "I have come many miles to ask you a question."

"Is that so?" I confess I have a weakness for flattery. I took the ring from him, unable to stop myself. It was a large piece of superior craftsmanship; though obviously several centuries old, it was in pristine condition. The jewel in the center of the ring was deep of hue and beautifully polished, and the thick gold band that housed the gem was expertly wrought with twin lion heads. It was marvelous; though my personal collection of jewelry, especially amethyst pieces, is extensive, I had never seen a piece so fine as that one.

"It is said your expertise in identifying gemstones is unrivalled," said Mr. Bernard. "I beg you to inspect this, which my uncle bequeathed to me on his deathbed. It is a family heirloom, and has a family legend, too."

I was very excited by this. At first glance, I would believe anything the man said about this ring, even if he claimed it belonged to a king or a saint; it really was remarkable. Holding it in my hand I was most impressed by its weight, but when I held it up to the light I was bewitched by the complexity of its luster and depth of color.

"Tell me the legend," I said, after begging Miss Mallory's pardon and excusing myself.

"If you will permit me an impertinence," he said, "let me first ask your first guess as to the ring's origin?"

"Spanish," I said immediately, certain I was correct. "It is obviously of Castilian craftsmanship."

Mr. Bernard smiled. "Indeed it is," he said. "I see the rumors of your authority are not at all exaggerated. Well, permit me a second impertinence—how old would you guess this ring is?"

"No older than the fourteenth century."

"Correct again." He smiled. "Do you know the legend of how Christopher Columbus came to finance his journey to the New World?"

"Queen Isabella pawned her gems," I breathed. My heart was pounding; I have rarely felt so excited.

"Don't tell me—"

"That story is not entirely true," interrupted Mr. Bernard. "Queen Isabella did indeed pawn her gems, but not for Señor Colón. No, the queen pawned her collection of jewels to finance the siege of Baeza, in Granada. This ring allegedly belonged to her, but was never recovered. It is said an ancestor of mine— an apprentice who worked for a jeweler—absconded with it, after the woman he loved, the daughter of that jeweler, named it as her bride price." Mr. Bernard shrugged. "Not the most honorable of legends, but after so many centuries I am willing to let bygones be bygones when it comes to family pride."

"Indeed," I said. "So why present this to me?"

"I was curious if you might be able to verify the story," replied Mr. Bernard.

"You came all this way to ask me?" I was flattered, but also surprised. "Surely an expert closer to your home would—"

"The band is undoubtedly from that time and place," he interrupted. "I am curious about the stone itself."

"Ah." I ran my finger over the gem. "Well…unfortunately, I must soon begin my concert. Perhaps later tonight, we might go to my rooms and discuss this matter further? I have certain philosophical and scientific apparatuses that would allow us to ascertain the truth of the matter."

"Fine, fine," said Mr. Bernard, looking very pleased indeed. Too pleased, perhaps—it made me wonder if his aim was truly finding out the origin of his peculiar gemstone.

Of course, we were long in getting to my chambers due to the unfortunate wager that resulted in your cousin's extreme agitation (and, if you are correct in your suspicions, eventual death). I shan't gloss over this, however, as I can use this opportunity to address your other concern: what exactly happened in the gardens.

Your confessing doubt in my magickal abilities does not offend me. I perfectly understand your desire to "see for yourself." These days it is increasingly fashionable to dismiss the arcane and esoteric in favor of the observable and mundane; or, I should say, what can be "proven" with modern science. This is nothing to me. Over the course of my life I have seen such great advancements in the philosophical realm. Matters which in previous centuries were viewed as impossible, or heretical—heliocentrism, for example—are now gaining worldwide acceptance as correct, and natural. I do not doubt that one day those who doubt my methods will be proven wrong and seen as backwards as those who once whipped their own backs in order to stave off the dreaded Pestilence. Yes, Mr. Bretwynde—what I am saying is that magick is every bit as real as anything mentioned in Sir Isaac Newton's *Principia*—and let us not forget that Newton, so popularly venerated today as a man of science, was also an alchemist and occult philosopher!

Newton is a good place to begin, actually. I know from our conversations that you are a learned man. Thus, you will concede that there are "laws of nature," as Newton himself sought to ascertain through his experiments. These laws, allegedly, are the underlying, unvarying uniformities of the world. Never will I drop an apple and it fall up, yes? Even if I believe as hard as I can that the apple will ascend, it never will.

Magick works differently. While I believe it will one day be proven to be a law such as gravity, currently no one has ascertained precisely how it works, and why. It also, unlike gravity, requires *belief.* The strength of any magickal work is entirely dependent upon the strength of faith of its creator—and, occasionally, its spectators.

Mr. Bretwynde, when I proposed the diversion in the gardens, it was with no hope that Mr. Welby might actually channel a god…and yet, that is what happened. The power of belief amongst your party must have tipped the scales tremendously—quite flattering, really—resulting in all that transpired. I promise you, I never intended to madden your poor fiancée with my efforts, and indeed, I never did. The god himself chose her as his acolyte for his own inscrutable reasons; if you wish the mental return of Miss Mallory I suggest you petition *him.* Your experience with the ancient world should indicate how best to proceed; I could recommend a few texts if you find yourself frustrated.

So there are your answers as regards what truly happened that night. To return to your foremost concern, however, I must skip disclosing any details of the ritual and begin with its aftermath, when Mr. Bernard refused the god's gift of ecstasy, and we retired to my rooms.

Once there, I began to set out my various alchemical devices, but Mr. Bernard, to my surprise, seemed less than interested. He wandered to and fro, picking up objects and setting them down again, humming to himself. He seemed startled when I asked him for the ring.

"Oh, yes," he said, and tossed it to me carelessly. "There you go. *Fais ce que tu voudras.*"

I did, and from what I ascertained from the carving and the setting of the piece, it could very well have belonged to Queen Isabella of Spain. I told him as much, and he nodded, as if this simply confirmed what he already knew. It was hardly, I noted, the reaction of a man who had journeyed far to obtain an answer.

"Do you like that ring, your Lordship?"

I laughed. "Yes, very much so, Mr. Bernard. It is beautiful beyond words, and rarer still. I am pleased you came all this way to show it to me. It is incomparable."

"Does that mean you possess nothing that is its equal?"

"Perhaps not," I said warily.

"Do you wish to possess it?"

I did not know how to respond. It was, I felt, impossible to accept such a priceless heirloom... but then again, this was a man who had just won an enormously profitable Jamaica plantation in a card game. He could afford to be generous. Even so, I was uncomfortable with the cavalier way he offered the ring to me. I did not recall him drinking much wine, so I did not think he was drunk. No; I was certain something else was going on, some subtext that I had yet to tease out.

"It is not for me to wish anything as regards the ownership of your ring," I said carefully.

"But it would enhance your collection?"

"Yes, it would." I saw no reason to lie.

"I will make you a present of it," he declared. "It is yours."

"I couldn't possibly." I stood, and walking over, set it on the arm of the chair in which Mr. Bernard lounged. "Thank you, but I must refuse."

"Why?" Mr. Bernard did not move to take back his ring. "What scruple could possibly prevent you from accepting it?"

I did not like this game. I am not a man to be toyed with. When I did not respond, Mr. Bernard laughed.

"Perhaps you do not like to receive something for nothing," he said. "Well, then! Give me something in exchange, a mere trifle to you, I am sure. Then your heart will be easy."

I have met many a charlatan in my day—have been rightfully accused of chicanery more than once—but never had I met such a bold-faced fraud as this Mr. Bernard. Even putting aside his dissembling with me, the stunt he pulled with your cousin at the card-table put him in the ranks of the few.

Yes, as a man of experience when it comes to these matters, the longer I associated with Mr. Bernard the more I found something repellant about him...and yet, I still found him enthralling. I have heard tell of animals being spellbound by the movements of predatory snakes; ever since that night, I have felt a kinship with those poor creatures, though I could not explain to you why. It amuses me that you chose to redact so-called ghastly and "unprovable" allegations against Mr. Bernard: I would believe anything you said about him, even if you alleged he was a demon walking the earth in the body of a man. The way he offered me the ring made me wonder if he would ask me if I would pledge my soul for it.

I decided, therefore, that the soundest way to deal with this individual was to be as direct as possible.

"What would you ask of me, Mr. Bernard? Be clear, please, and more direct than you have been."

Mr. Bernard stood and walked over to my window, where he looked down onto the gardens. "The Count of St. Germain is known for many things," he said softly, so softly I could not help drawing nearer to him to hear all he said. "His obsession with gems, his violin-playing—and his immortality."

"Ah." I could not help but smile, and felt more at ease than I had previously. "You come seeking the philosopher's stone, or the Elixir of Life, or whatever it is you think I possess to remain eternally young. You think to bribe me with something you believe I cannot resist. I have been offered more than jewelry for the secret. Let me warn you now, no matter how hard you press me, you will come away disappointed."

Just then, we both heard a scream that came from the direction of the gardens. I glanced at the window, but assumed it was simply a part of the ongoing bacchanal. Mr. Bernard did not seem to heed it, either.

"You do not like me." There was no rancor in Mr. Bernard's voice. "Well, your Lordship, what if I promised you that this thing I seek, it is not for myself, but for another. I have no personal interest in your secret; no need for what you possess."

"I cannot help you," I said. "I am sorry, Mr. Bernard. Take back your ring, find some other way to pass your night. Join the revels below, retire to your rooms...whatever you please."

Mr. Bernard sighed. "I was afraid the ring would not be enough incentive to convince you," he said. "I suppose I must offer to relieve you of something rather than give you something, in order to obtain what I want."

A second scream wafted up to us from the gardens, chilling me in equal measure to what Mr. Bernard had just said. I wondered if I oughtn't go down there to see what was going on, but I had a significantly more pressing concern at that moment which required my full attention. The hairs were standing on the back of my neck; again, I felt that sense of being in the presence of something dangerous, an inhuman and unpredictable creature.

"You're threatening me." We were standing side by side, looking down into the gardens. "You think if I fear for my life, the thing you believe I possess in infinite quantities, then I will divulge what you seek. Well, Mr. Bernard—I say, is that..."

Below us, and outside, a slender figure had just dashed out of the house toward the gardens. It was Dionysios. Mr. Bernard inhaled sharply—not quite a gasp, but close to it—as the boy pelted toward the entrance of the maze. But Mr. Bernard became more obviously agitated when your friend Mr. James bolted into the light and bowled Dionysios over. When Mr. Welby launched himself over the edge of the maze, not even using his hands, just by the strength of his legs, followed closely by a bloodied and ululating Miss Mallory, his attention was sufficiently redirected that I no longer worried he would attack me.

"I must go," he said, and fled my room. I followed him, though I wished I did not feel compelled to do so. But I could not leave Mr. James to the tender mercies of two individuals who were entheos or enraptured in some way; their situation was due in part to my appeal to Bacchus, and thus I felt some sense of responsibility.

By the time we arrived at the scene, Dionysios was nowhere to be found, and your fiancée had already begun her assault. Unable to deal with Miss Mallory alone, I was forced to call upon Mr. Bernard to assist me. I am not the strongest of men, and her vigor was prodigious that night, given its source. Mr. Bernard, however, was somehow able to restrain Miss Mallory as I dealt with Mr. Welby, who was more amenable to exercising restraint after I formally petitioned that which wore his skin, the details of which I shall spare you. But knowing your former relationship with Miss Mallory, I would have you know I did ask for her wherewithal to be returned—but sadly, it was judged impossible, as she had given of herself voluntarily. Whether that means she may one day return to you is beyond my knowledge; I hope at least you take comfort knowing she made the choice that has resulted in her confinement, rather than it being a fate foisted upon her.

In the end, Mr. Bernard and I put Miss Mallory into a closet where she would not endanger herself or others, and returned Mr. Welby to his rooms where we poured him a large brandy upon his coming back to himself. As he drank it down in large gulps, Mr. Bernard excused himself, citing a wish to find his manservant and depart from Tarrington.

"I know he will not want to see me," he murmured in my ear, "and I believe you and I have nothing more to say to one another."

"Not much more," I replied, "but some. Go—I will catch up."

As he shut the door behind him, Mr. Welby sat up straight.

"That man! It was Mr. Bernard!"

"Calm yourself, Mr. Welby," I said, in soothing tones. "You have been through an ordeal."

"I must catch him and speak with him," insisted Mr. Welby. "Please, sir, let me up, let me go!"

"You must rest yourself. Mr. Bernard is seeing to his own affairs, as you must to yours. While he means to leave Tarrington, surely he does not mean to do so right this instant—"

"I'm jolly well certain he does!" Mr. Welby was on his feet, running to the door. "The villain will be preparing as we speak! Perhaps if I go to his rooms I shall find him..."

And then he was gone. Knowing that Mr. Bernard would not go to his rooms, but outside in pursuit of

Dionysios, I tracked him thence, and told him what Mr. Welby had vowed, not wishing either to have the advantage on the other. While I did not like Mr. Bernard, neither did I wish to see him murdered.

Mr. Bernard, for his part, seemed unsurprised. "His dismay is to be expected. He did lose most of what he owned this night. Ah, well, it is nothing to me—and look there, it is my man," he said, pointing to where two figures—yourself, and Dionysios—stood at the entrance to your maze. "Good evening, your Lordship. I regret we were not able to do business with one another…tonight."

The way he said it chilled me, but I would not show that to him.

"We will *never* do business, on any night," I assured him. "I am not able to give you the secret, or any man. It is not mine to give, please understand."

"As you will." He did not sound convinced. "Perhaps one day—if you are truthful about your own abilities—we shall meet again. It may be that at such a time you will be less averse." He smiled. "I have left the ring in your room. Consider it an advance on your eventual amenability. Good evening, your Lordship."

"Mr. Bernard, you mistake my resolve. I—"

"As I said, *good evening.*"

That, Mr. Bretwynde, is why I felt a sense of relief, *joy*, even, upon receiving your letter, though it was with a heavy heart that I read most of what you had to say. Hearing Mr. Bernard has gone to Jamaica will allow me to rest more easily. He does not seem the sort of man to fail to make good on a promise.

I will depart soon—your letter caught me just before I take my leave, in fact. I am glad you found me, but do not seek to again. While you may hear tell of me in the coming years, do not look for me where I am said to be. I shall say no more, save to comment that being in the public eye is often the safest place for someone wishing to hide. With that, I bid you *adieu*, Mr. Bretwynde. I hope what I have communicated here will be of some help to you.

Yours—

***

The letter was, of course, unsigned.

This is the last I shall allow myself to write on the intriguing matter of the Count of St. Germain's visit to Tarrington House or the repercussions of that strange night. Any will I once possessed to continue my researches has been swept away by the Count's letter. His words—bah! I had hoped that he would say something on Mr. Bernard's behalf that would allow me to completely dismiss Chidike's story…and yet, without his possessing any knowledge of what the poor man alleged, the Count in many ways served to validate the description of Mr. Bernard's devilishness.

Well, perhaps. Perhaps he was simply toying with me. I cannot credit St. Germain's account of the reality of "magick," and its peculiar if necessary reliance on human belief, and yet his words make me wonder. Certainly the existence of occult or extramundane things in this world would make for an easier explanation of what happened that night, but at the same time I feel I walk the path of madness to consider such a possibility. Frankly, it is maddening enough to think that while all my life I have longed to travel, to see the world, such strangeness could occur in my own back yard…and that I would miss it entirely, only learning of its existence after the fact.

No; in the end, I cannot dismiss the option that the Count was merely continuing his performance, especially in light of him promising he would recommend me certain books to help Phylotha—and then telling me not to seek him out, nor providing me a forwarding address! And, I should add, telling me I should not mourn, for she *chose* her path! What does that mean, exactly? That she preferred to live insane and isolated rather than marry me?[4] Knowing my eagerness to see some real magic, does he mean to make me feel even more culpable, saying it was the strength of the belief of those watching him—myself included—that produced such dramatic and unusual results? I already feel so much crushing guilt over everything that I am a very Atlas under its weight—a pebble more would be my undoing.

How infuriating, that after compiling these accounts of what others remember, and writing down all I can personally recall, I remain confounded. I must conclude there are no real answers to my questions.

Perhaps I am being too hard on myself. It is not, after all, that I have obtained no answers. No, the problem is that I have most of those answers, but now possess a host of other doubts, commonplace and esoteric. Did Phylotha love me? Is magic real—and did it manifest that night? Did Chidike really witness some sort

---

4. Regardless, I have begun combing my modest classical library in the hopes I shall find some way of rescuing Phylotha from her madness, if indeed she wishes to be rescued. If I am able to discover any thing that will help her, and, if the Count's word is to be trusted, believe in whatever I find, perhaps our respective futures need not be so lonely. I liked Miss Mallory before I loved her, and I do not dismiss that such might be possible once again, even knowing she spoke unkind words about me to another. But what am I saying—if I am able to aid her recovery, even if she never wishes to see me again, I shall consider my time well spent. —J.B.

of necromantic diabolism, or was he exhausted and confused? Was Vandeleur playing along at the ceremony, or was he truly channeling a god?

And *you*, Dionysios…what of you? You most beautiful, most dear, most perplexing of creatures…you who bewitch me still, though I doubt your honesty as much as your innocence, and for that matter your humanity. Were you sincere with me at any point, about your feelings for me, or any other thing? If you were to read this, what sensations would you feel? Would you laugh? Shed a tear? Would you feel a pang in your empty breast over your heartless deceptions—or reach out to me once again to assure me of your affections?

No! I must stop. I am forced, at last, to agree with the Lady Nerissa, first of my correspondents. Mulling over these odd events has not made me happier. It has cost me more time, energy, health, and heartache than I ever should have allowed, and proven only that I am a fool. While I believe a part of me will always yearn to know what on earth really transpired at that fateful gathering, I must put it from my mind. I will never be able to ascertain the truth. Of that, and that alone, am I certain.

"…prepare to be shocked, charmed, and (somewhat moistly) entertained!" —Livia Llewellyn, author of *Furnace*

A Pretty Mouth

Molly Tanzer

The Molly Tanzer Collection

A faithful valet is forced into the service of a decadent lord. A young writer of erotica returns to the family estate after many years in exile. A pair of twins conspires to explore the most eldritch and macabre debaucheries. A troupe of soldiers face off against unimagined barbarity. A young man determines to be part of the in crowd… at any cost.

From Molly Tanzer comes *A Pretty Mouth*, an interlaced collection detailing the triumphs and misadventures of the decadent Calipash dynasty, a family blessed—and cursed— by cosmic weirdness.

Format: Trade Paperback, 270 pp, $17.99

ISBN-13: 978-1-939905-62-8

http://www.wordhorde.com

"...completely captivating from start to finish, Tanzer's The Pleasure Merchant is the very best sort of literature: a rare pleasure indeed. —*Electric Literature*

When apprentice wig-maker Tom Dawne's greatest creation is used as part of a revenge scheme against a powerful gentleman, he is dismissed by his embarrassed master and forced to abandon his dreams of completing his training, setting up a shop of his own, and marrying his master's daughter. Determined to clear his name, Tom becomes the servant of the man he suspects set him up. Tom finds himself caught up in a web of ambition, deceit, mesmerism, sex, and power... and at its center, a man able to procure pleasure for anyone–for a price–and a woman whose past has been stolen.

Format: Trade Paperback, 348 pp, $17.99

ISBN-13: 978-1-939905-66-6

http://www.wordhorde.com

"…an excellent read for those who enjoy myths and legends of all kinds." —*Publishers Weekly* (starred review)

For a decade, author Christine Morgan's Viking stories have delighted readers and critics alike, standing apart from the anthologies they appeared in. Now, Word Horde brings you *The Raven's Table*, the first-ever collection of Christine Morgan's Vikings, from "The Barrow-Maid" to "Aerkheim's Horror" and beyond. These tales of adventure, fantasy, and horror will rouse your inner Viking.

"…stories that will make you want to don your helm, sword and shield before riding off into battle." —*The Grim Reader*

Format: Trade Paperback, 306 pp, $16.99

ISBN-13: 978-1-939905-68-0

http://www.wordhorde.com

"Infused with mythology and magic, these dark tales cast a powerful spell." —*Publishers Weekly*

For more than a decade, author Christine Morgan's Viking stories have delighted readers and critics, standing apart from the anthologies they appeared in. Now, Word Horde brings you *The Wolf's Feast*, a new collection of Christine Morgan's Vikings, from "The Viking in Yellow" to "Odin's Eagle" and beyond. These tales of adventure, fantasy, and horror will be sure to rouse your inner Viking.

Format: Trade Paperback, 326 pp, $16.99
ISBN-13: 978-1-939905-58-1
http://www.wordhorde.com

About the Author

Molly Tanzer is the author of the Diabolist's Library trilogy: *Creatures of Will and Temper*, the *Locus* Award-nominated *Creatures of Want and Ruin*, and *Creatures of Charm and Hunger*. She is also the author of the weird western *Vermilion*, an io9 and NPR "Best Book" of 2015, and the British Fantasy Award-nominated collection, *A Pretty Mouth*. Her critically acclaimed short fiction has appeared in *The Magazine of Fantasy and Science Fiction*, *Lightspeed*, *Transcendent: The Year's Best Trans and Nonbinary Speculative Fiction*, and elsewhere. Follow her on Instagram @molly_tanzer or @wickedmilkhotel on Twitter. She lives outside of Boulder, CO with her cat, Toad.